MORTAL PASSION

By the same author

HOW TO BE AN ALIEN
HOW TO BE INIMITABLE
HOW TO SCRAPE SKIES
WISDOM FOR OTHERS
MILK AND HONEY
EAST IS EAST
DOWN WITH EVERYBODY!
SHAKESPEARE AND MYSELF
ÜBER ALLES
EIGHT HUMORISTS
LITTLE CABBAGES
ITALY FOR BEGINNERS
TANGO
SWITZERLAND FOR BEGINNERS

★

THE HUNGARIAN REVOLUTION
A STUDY IN INFAMY

GEORGE MIKES

Mortal Passion

CONTEMPORARY FICTION
ANDRE DEUTSCH
London 1965

This Contemporary Fiction edition was produced in 1965 for sale to its members only by the proprietors, Readers Union Ltd, at Aldine House, 10-13 Bedford Street, London W.C.2 and at Letchworth Garden City, Herts. Full details of membership may be obtained from our London address. The book is set in 11 point Imprint type, and has been reprinted by Ebenezer Baylis & Son Ltd, Worcester. It was first published by André Deutsch Limited.

To my daughter
Judy
who does not think much of writers.
But this is not the only
thing we have in common

NOTE

I know that some readers with a knowledge of Hungarian will cry out about the lack of accents on some vowels. I have chucked them deliberately; I meant to make it easier for the English reader.

G.M.

CONTENTS

TWO SCHEMES

I was sitting in my room, number 2334, on the 23rd floor of the Potomac Hotel, 26th Street East, New York, thinking gratefully of Miss Eleanor Sputz. I had just returned from Allyears, the publishers. On my arrival there, a lady who, to judge from her uniform, could have been an elderly lift-girl, but who, from her imperious manners, might have been the Chairman's eldest daughter, told me: 'Miss Sputz will be with you presently.'

'Miss Sputz?' I asked with some uncertainty in my voice.

'Miss Eleanor Sputz,' she repeated curtly. 'She's your editor.'

I did not know what an editor was; still less did I know that I had one. But if Miss Sputz was my editor, then that was that and all I could say was 'Oh yes . . .' and wait for Miss Sputz. I settled down in a circular ante-room, the walls of which were covered with books, all Allyears publications. A synthetic blonde sat behind a desk laden with an array of telephones. She threw an unfriendly glance in my direction and went on polishing her fingernails. Men and women dashed periodically across the room, shouting 'Hiyah Gertrude', 'Hiyah John', 'Hiyah Elmer' and ignoring me as if to say 'We are members of a famous fraternity, a happy, important band of people, but we don't know you.' Suddenly Gertrude, the receptionist, Myrna, with whom she was now chatting, and John, who was listening in, jumped to their feet and shouted with somewhat artificial enthusiasm: 'Oh, Mr Vice-President . . . good morning to you.' 'Hiyah girls,' said the Vice-President, which John must have found a trifle disconcerting but if he did, he gave no sign of his feelings. 'Has the . . . what's his name . . . has the

Duke of Wiltshire called with a parcel, Gertrude?' 'No, he hasn't, Mr Vice-President,' replied Gertrude. 'You bet he hasn't,' I murmured. The next moment the Vice-President was gone, leaving a faint aura of greatness behind him. Gertrude threw another superior and contemptuous glance at me. Then in came an elderly Negro charwoman in a bright uniform, looking like a rear-admiral in a newly organised African navy, carrying two shining buckets and she, too, said 'Hiyah Gertrude'. 'Hiyah Alice,' Gertrude replied and then the telephone rang.

'Mr Matyas,' Gertrude turned to me. She was all well-rehearsed, cool yet friendly efficiency now.

'Yes,' I said.

'Miss Sputz is ready for you.'

I was led into Miss Sputz's room, or rather cage. The immensity of floor-space at Allyears is divided by wooden partitions into hundreds of little cages. I rather expected curt notices: DO NOT FEED THE EDITORS. THEY HAVE A SPECIAL DIET, ON EXPENSE ACCOUNTS.

Miss Sputz was a meticulously dressed and coiffured young lady. At first I thought she was twelve; later, however, I found out that she was a college graduate, so I reckoned that she must be at least fourteen.

'Pleased to meet you, Mr Matyas,' she said. She spoke in staccato sentences and with great self-assurance. 'We don't like your book.'

'Oh . . .' said I.

'No, we don't like it at all. We don't like your style. We don't like your subject. Your jokes are laboured. We don't like your characters.'

I waited patiently for Miss Sputz to tell me what else she did not like, but that was all.

'But that wouldn't really matter much,' she continued.

'Wouldn't it?' I asked, a little surprised.

'No, that wouldn't in itself. But your book is much too British.'

'*My* book? Too British?'

'Much too British,' Miss Sputz repeated her verdict severely.

'You know, of course,' I said, 'that I am only a naturalised British subject and that I used to be a Hungarian refugee?'

'We know that.'

'Yet, my book is much too English?'

'That's the main trouble with it,' Miss Sputz declared grimly.

'Don't you publish some of Sir Winston Churchill's works?'

'We are proud to have published one or two of his books,' Miss Sputz consented with great dignity.

'And he wasn't too English for you ?'

'Sir Churchill's books are all right in every respect,' she informed me coolly.

'But mine . . .'

'Yours is much too English,' she insisted. 'But you show a certain amount of talent, Mr Matyas. Don't let yourself get discouraged. Go on writing. One day you might become a little less English and then, I am sure, you will produce a book which Allyears will take. In the meantime should you ever need guidance and advice, you know where to find me.'

That indicated that my audience with Miss Sputz was over, so I left. It was this conversation which cheered me up no end. My fourteen previous books had sold over a million copies in twenty-three languages; I had won the Esther L. Popplewell Prize (£15 in cash and a photograph, personally signed by Elza L. Popplewell—Esther L. Popplewell's niece); and now that charming, earnest teenager, Miss Sputz, was encouraging me to go on writing. Alas, I thought, even had she sought to dissuade me, I no longer had any choice. It is difficult enough to become a writer; but much more difficult to cease being one.

'She is my editor,' I mused, lying on the sofa in my hotel

room. 'But why do I need an editor if they don't want to publish my book? What is she going to edit?'

The telephone rang. It was the hall porter.

'Mr MacKay is here,' he said. He pronounced the name in the American way, making *kay* rhyme with *hay*.

'MacKay?' said I. 'I'm not expecting any MacKay.'

'I didn't say you were. All I said he's here,' the porter replied with the inimitable courtesy of American hotel employees and with admirable logic.

'A Scotsman?' I said inquiringly.

'I wouldn't say so,' he answered and I thought I discerned amusement in his voice.

'Send him up.'

'Nice to meet you, Mr Matyas,' said Mr MacKay in Hungarian, entering my room. He was a man of about forty, slightly plump, with a round friendly face and a twinkle in his eye. He was extremely un-Scottish—even in a kilt I should have taken him, without a moment's hesitation, for a Central European refugee. 'I am a friend . . .' and he mentioned the name of an old London friend. 'He told me . . .'

'Before we go into all that,' said I, trying not to sound abrupt, 'would you care to explain to me how you got hold of the name MacKay?'

'Oh that . . . Simply because that's always been my name. I used to spell it *Makkai* which, as you know, is a fairly common name in Hungary. In England, where I lived for a while, people pronounced it correctly in the Hungarian way, I mean, making the *kai* rhyme with *I*, but they kept on telling me that I was spelling it wrongly. Here in America people changed the pronunciation and started spelling it *MacKay* without any further ado and against all my protestations. So what could I do? I gave in.'

'But that's an ancient Scottish name,' I told him.

'That's between the Americans and the Celts. Do you want a cigarette?'

'That depends. What do you smoke?'

He smoked Chesterfields and that being my brand, I accepted one. There are only four or five popular brands in the United States but, funnily enough, this was the very first occasion that anyone offered me a brand I smoked myself.

Mr MacKay—Sam, as he told me his friends called him—eventually broached the reason for his visit.

'Are you corrupt?' he asked me.

'I have always wanted to be,' I replied, 'but have never had much luck. Nobody has ever wanted to bribe me.'

'Here's your great chance. Do you know Borsch?'

'Well . . . yes,' said I, now really taken aback. I knew Borsch in London, shortly before the outbreak of the war. He was then a shabbily dressed man of limited intelligence—an engineer of sorts—and I always tried to avoid him because he kept touching everybody for small sums. As I cannot say 'No' to anyone, Borsch cost me quite a lot of money at a time when I did not have too much of it. I knew that later he had done quite well—indeed I had heard that he had become a millionaire.

Yes, I had known Borsch quite well but I had not thought of him for fourteen years. I had almost forgotten his very existence.

'Do you know him well?' Sam inquired.

'I used to know him quite well. But I haven't seen him since 1941, when I visited him in the internment camp, on the Isle of Man. That was fourteen years ago.'

'You actually visited him in the camp? That's good.' Sam was pleased. 'Now listen. The bribe is this: I introduce you to Sasdy —head of the Hungarian desk at the "Soul of the United States" Radio Station. You can, I'm sure, write a talk for them. They pay fabulously. And you, in turn, introduce me to Borsch. O.K.?'

I was disappointed. I had expected something darker and more intriguing than a double introduction. But after my mishap with Allyears, the fee for the talk would come in handy.

'It's a deal,' I nodded and we shook hands.

15

He asked me what I was doing right then and I told him that I was free for an hour or so. He suggested that we should go out for a walk and discuss strategy. We walked around, mapping out our plan; who should contact whom and when. We found ourselves in front of Pennsylvania Railroad Station and we walked in. Glass doors opened automatically as we approached them, people—mostly without luggage—were rushing about in all directions, jostling and pushing us aside, occasionally murmuring 'Pardon me' which, to my ears, always sounded more like a swear-word or a threat than an apology. There was a fat lady throwing innumerable one-cent pieces into a postal franking machine. A youth was trying to fit a large suitcase into one of those small steel cupboards which are used as automatic cloakrooms. We walked along the corridor and passed the subway entrance; there was a dazzlingly illuminated bookshop on our right and an even more dazzlingly illuminated drug-store on our left. We passed a few establishments where Negro men and women were serving sizzling hot frankfurters, hamburgers and what are known as cheeseburgers to morose, ill-tempered customers who ate them standing up and drank yellow and green liquids from paper tumblers to wash them down. We reached a cheap but inviting restaurant. Sam suddenly stopped talking and gave his attention to a close examination of the menu which was pinned up in a small glass cage. I asked him something but he did not seem to hear me.

'Let's have some oysters,' he suggested. He sounded rather grim and determined, I thought.

'Let's,' said I. I am never against having oysters; besides, I felt a strange urgency in Sam's voice and I felt it would be wrong to refuse.

We went in, sat down at a well-polished wooden table in the shadow of a gigantic sugar-sifter, and picked up the huge, glossy, coloured price-list. They had eight kinds of oysters.

'Half a dozen Blue Points for me,' I said to the waitress. She nodded and looked at Sam.

'Yes . . . Blue Points will do,' he said thoughtfully.
'Six or a dozen?' asked the waitress impatiently.
'Neither,' replied Sam. 'I'll take three dozen.'
I thought he was joking.

But he was in dead earnest. He had his three dozen Blue Points—served in huge platters, brought to him one after the other—and went on, rather thoughtfully, discussing Borsch and my talk for the 'Soul of the United States'.

2

The first leg of our joint enterprise was only a qualified success.

Miklos Sasdy, one of the assistants of the Hungarian desk at the 'Soul of the United States' Radio Station seemed to like the idea of my giving a gay, lighthearted talk on my impressions of New York. I could write whatever I wanted, he told me on the phone, and he hoped, indeed, that this went without saying; America was a free country and I could express my views freely. Of course, I should not criticise New York because this broadcast would be listened to by millions behind the Iron Curtain and there was not much point in running down the greatest American city in earshot of the Communists—although, he added, all their listeners were anti-Communists. But as long as I said nothing critical of, or jocular about, New York and its way of life, I could speak as freely as I wished. Although this was a lighthearted talk, he explained—an entertainment, if I did not mind him saying so—and not a political lecture, I was just as free to express my political views as all others. Did I, for example, want to attack Senator McCarthy? Well, I should just go ahead. Not because the Senator had become a dead duck by now, whom no one took seriously. Oh no, I must not think that. This was just one aspect of absolute freedom. In fact— Mr Sasdy went on—far from keeping away from politics, he would be grateful if I mentioned three small points in that light-hearted, entertaining talk of mine on New York: (1) how grateful all Europeans were to America's great President, Dwight D. Eisenhower; (2) what a truly great man Secretary of State John Foster Dulles was; (3) the summit meeting which the Russians, supported by the British, were pressing for, was not a good idea and I had gained the impression, moving about in the City of New York, that the population was unanimously against bargaining with the Reds.

When Sam noticed that a last feeble flicker of integrity made me toy with the idea of chucking the whole project, he remarked: 'They pay fabulously, don't forget that. Two hundred dollars for a talk. And unlike your famous B.B.C., they don't send you a cheque weeks and weeks later: they pay you on the spot. In cash.'

The word 'cash' settled my doubts and I sat down to write my talk as instructed. Later, Mr Sasdy rang me up to say that a change had occurred in America's attitude towards the planned summit and would I please say that my little chats with the men in the street had convinced me that the people of New York were warm-heartedly behind the idea of a summit meeting. I asked him whether, instead of speaking of 'reds', I might refer to the Russians as 'our former allies'? He said that would be O.K.

Sam warned me that a certain amount of tact was required when dealing with the people in the Hungarian service of the 'Soul of the United States'. The present lot were the fifth set of employees. The first set—consisting mostly of former Horthyite army officers and civil servants—were all fired one day by the Americans as dangerous liberals and left-wing agitators and replaced by ex-members of the pro-Nazi Arrow Cross party. At the height of the McCarthy purges, the Nazis were kicked out as Communist sympathisers, and even their American bosses were dismissed for having employed them. One of the new Hungarians, who followed, a former colonel of the gendarmerie, was not a bright man so he seemed to be all right for the job. Nevertheless, he fell victim to the only bright remark he ever made in his life. He said—no one knew if seriously, jocularly, or just repeating something he had heard from others —that he was puzzled by the sackings that had preceded him as he had always understood that American policy in Eastern Europe was based on the support of repentant Communists and unrepentant Nazis. This remark—like everything else— was reported to the Americans, so the colonel of gendarmerie was sacked. Disgusted with politics and what he called intellectual life, he opened a butcher's shop, sold Hungarian sausages and other specialities, did a roaring trade and enjoyed the support of all Hungarians whatever their politics. The fourth lot at the 'Soul' was sacked *in toto* on moral grounds, when three secretaries found themselves pregnant, by one of the translators, a former priest, now a lay preacher. As the third of these girls was an American, he was declared a Fifth Amendment Communist and fired on political grounds. Then came Sasdy's lot. He had been a clerk in the Dry Fodder Department of the Hungarian Ministry of Agriculture and all seemed well with his boys. The atmosphere of the place—according to Sam—was about as inspiring as a provincial tax collector's office with a spot of undertaking thrown in, but work proceeded with great bureaucratic efficiency and all talks once broadcast were properly filed.

The other trouble was, Sam explained, that the place had become a hot-bed of intrigue. From past experience it was found to be prudent to live in daily expectation of instant dismissal, so everyone watched everyone else, kept their ears open for hasty and thoughtless remarks, and collected compromising material wherever found about superiors as well as colleagues and underlings. Many a chance remark was jotted down with a stub of pencil in a little red notebook, in the hope that its author might thereby be revealed as a Communist spy. All courtships, liaisons and suspected affairs were also duly recorded in these top-secret files. All the same, it was well known that the lists were no good. There were too many of them and, in their totality, they cancelled each other out; if they proved anything at all, it was that *everybody* was a bolshevik agent and a sexual pervert. While these preparations were going ahead in secret, however, the atmosphere above board seemed pleasant enough, and friendly.

I personally fared reasonably well. The single change they requested me to make in my script was to condemn the idea of a summit meeting because, that morning, they were dead set against it. After the recording, Mr Sasdy assured me that my piece was excellent, that it would create quite a stir in Hungary. He shook me warmly by the hand and saw me to the door.

'You've got my address?' I asked him uncertainly. 'Potomac Hotel.'

'Yes, I've got it,' he said amiably, 'but I don't think I'll need it.'

'Well,' I said feeling more and more lost, 'if you want to send me a cheque or something.'

'A cheque?' he exclaimed. He acted as though I had used a very dirty word. 'A cheque? But we always pay cash.'

'I see . . .' said I, feeling a little more hopeful.

Then he explained, earnestly: 'It's like this. Right through the year, we always pay our contributors. In fact, we pay very well. But by March we always run out of funds and we don't get a cent till April. So in March we can't pay. It sounds crazy. Bad luck you come along in March.'

'Yes, it *is* rather bad luck,' I remarked thoughtfully. 'You don't think you could borrow something from next year's budget?'

That startled him.

'Next year's budget?' He looked as if I had tempted him to commit a crime. His expression spoke more clearly than his voice: to borrow from next year's budget was practically stealing; to send me away without paying me a cent was, apparently, the only decent thing to do.

'You don't want me to give another talk in April if I'm still here?' I suggested tentatively.

'No, thanks. You have just given your impressions of New York. You won't have any new impressions by April.'

I told him that I was gathering new impressions all the time. I had just gathered some brand new ones right there.

'But please don't take this as meaning that we didn't like your talk, because we did.'

I felt proud.

I met Sam in a nearby drug-store and told him what had happened. He looked embarrassed and started doodling on a paper serviette.

'Funny . . .' he said, and went on doodling. 'However, I assure you,' he said later, '*when* they do pay, they pay fabulously.'

He offered me a cigarette. When he handed me the little carton, I noticed it was Lucky Strike, so I lit one of my own and asked him why he'd given up Chesterfields.

'I had to,' he said, unhappily. 'I prefer Chesterfields. I don't like Lucky Strikes at all. But in the train every morning I can't see anything but Lucky Strike advertisements. They wore me down. My nerves couldn't stand it. Every time I lit a Chesterfield, I felt like a traitor. I became shaky. I threw my hand in. I'm smoking Lucky Strike now like they do in the advertisement. Guy can't always do what he likes.'

Thinking back on this, I find it rather endearing and typical of Sam. He had been bullied into using a name he did not quite accept, and smoking a brand of cigarettes he did not want to smoke. But right then and there I was not in the mood to be too understanding with him. I stared hard at what he was doodling.

'What on earth is that supposed to be?'

'Legs and breasts,' he replied guiltily.

'You dirty old man.'

He shook his head sadly.

'I'm not. I wish I were.'

After a moment's pause he added: 'I am drawing *chicken*

legs.' And with an almost lyrical softness in his voice, he added: 'And *chicken* breasts.'

I looked at the drawings and I looked at him. No explanations were forthcoming. All he said after a while, was: 'Well, I've kept my side of the bargain. You had your broadcast. It's your turn now to keep *your* promise. Take me to Borsch.'

'Yes,' I replied. 'Fair is fair.'

3

On the rather old-fashioned little Long Island train taking us to Port Washington, where Borsch lived, Sam was noticeably excited.

'You mustn't forget you are fighting for a principle,' he warned me. 'The principle being that I must have a job. I am not fussy but I need some kind of livelihood. It's better for humanity if I'm alive than if I starve to death. So in the sacred cause of humanity, try to pull it off.'

'In the sacred cause of humanity I'll try to squeeze as much money out of Borsch as my abilities and power of persuasion permit.'

Sam had told me that he had once had a most lucrative job at the State Department in Washington, as an expert on Czecho-Slovak affairs.

'It was inevitable,' he explained. 'Being a Hungarian, I know a little bit about all the neighbouring countries, with the single exception of Czecho-Slovakia. So it *had* to be Czecho-Slovakia.'

His ignorance of the subject stood him in good stead: his rise was rapid and spectacular. Nor did McCarthy harm him: when people were losing their jobs left and right, he indeed expected to be dismissed from one day to the next; but he never was. But when all the danger seemed to have abated, redundancy experts were sent round the various departments and they recommended his dismissal. Sam felt deeply aggrieved on this score. Not that he was not redundant; but, he felt, he was not *more* redundant than the overwhelming majority. His redundancy was just average, so why pick on him? But there was no appeal, he had to go; the State Department was determined to cut down expenses. Unexpectedly he received various payments, benefits, refunds and compensations, the equivalent of about two years' salary (which was one way of cutting down expenses, as the State Department understood it). Secure in possession of his large sum, Sam was at the moment better off than he had ever been in all his life. But he had to bear his future in mind.

Sam's simple idea was that Borsch be prevailed upon to support a small émigré monthly, to be edited by Sam. The whole scheme was to be managed on a shoe-string—indeed, half a shoe-string. All Sam wanted was 300 dollars a month. His flat, or 'apartment', was to serve as editorial office; contributors would all be devoted to the cause—in other words, they would not be paid. He knew a small printer who would do the job badly but cheaply—and there would be practically no expenses over and above printing and distribution. It could just be done on 300 dollars per issue. Sam's hope was that he might get together a few hundred subscribers, and also that he might be able to talk a few Hungarian business people (grocers who sold Hungarian sausages, spices and cheeses; 'patisserie-makers' who baked Hungarian cakes; vendors of Hungarian books and gramophone records, etc, etc) into advertising. He reckoned that the subscription fees plus the advertising revenue would be enough for him to live on—if Borsch paid all the printing and postal expenses.

Sam had very clear ideas as to the content of his magazine. By now he had told me these ideas in detail and I was somewhat surprised to see that he really believed in them. The magazine was to be called *A Hid*, which means *The Bridge*, and while it was to be uncompromising towards the baser tricks of Communism, it would advocate cessation of the cold war instead of fanning its flames. Central Europe must be free of Soviet domination, he said, but must remain friendly to the Soviet Union as the Russians could not be expected to tolerate a hostile base on their doorsteps. Further—and this was his pet idea—the magazine would fight for the collaboration, or eventual unity, of the Danubian peoples—Austrians, Czechs, Hungarians, Yugoslavs and Poles (the last appointed honorary Danubians by Sam). Sitting in the train, I listened at length to enthusiastic and imaginative schemes about an eventual Danubian Common Market; and was told serenely and emphatically that for those states a Confederation was to be preferred to a Federation. As I saw no immediate urgency in deciding this particular point, I asked Sam if I could return to this subject when it arose. Federation or Confederation, the immediate task seemed to my prosaic mind to be to persuade Borsch to cough up 300 dollars per month.

'You must handle him carefully,' Sam warned me again. 'He has certain weak spots. One is his sister, Mrs Doros, the widow of Leo Doros, the well-known speculator, share-pusher, usurer, realtor and thief. You must have known him well.'

'The truth is that I have the honour of knowing almost every Hungarian crook but I missed Leo Doros.'

'He was a bastard. After cheating and ruining folk in his office all day long, grabbing what he could by fair means or foul—nearly always foul—he'd go home and write sentimental poetry about orphans freezing to death in the snow and dicky birds not getting enough to eat in winter. His poetry was all brotherly love and patriotism with a lot of noble virgins pining away and brave soldiers falling in battle. And, of course, plenty of moonshine. Unfortunately, editors of the émigré Press were dependent on Doros's real-estate advertisements and they knew they couldn't get them without printing his poems about starving blackbirds and limping bees. By the way, all the birds in Long Island get so much to eat—summer and winter—that they can't fly and 32.7 per cent of them die of coronary thrombosis, caused by overeating.'

Sam offered me a Chesterfield. I regarded this as a personal compliment: for my sake, it seemed, he was, after all, prepared to out-face those menacing advertisements. He went on: 'Doros was an absolute swine to his wife, too. He had innumerable mistresses and seduced all his secretaries. Finally his wife made him engage a one-legged woman of fifty-four as his secretary. He seduced her too. In fact, he was madly in love with her for a while because, he said, that missing leg excited him frantically. He'd try to kiss any female visitor between the ages of nine and ninety. Then he'd get them to help in the kitchen so's he could get a handful of bosom when they were carrying trays. He always said women would put up with anything rather than drop a tray. Once he got his face slapped by his own cousin, a young woman of twenty-two, and that happened in the presence of eighteen other guests. Another time he had to beat it out of a restaurant on 49th Street on account of playing with a dame's knee and this dame he didn't really know. He left his wife three times to go and live with various women but he always forgave her—sure, sure you heard me—*he* always forgave *her*—and returned to the family hearth. Two years ago he tells Matilda, his wife, he has to go to Chicago for a realtors' convention and a couple of days later they ring Leo's wife up to say Leo's got himself a heart attack, in bed, in Atlantic City, with a lift-girl from the office, and Leo's dead. So Mrs Doros has her Leo's body brought home. This is the one time she knows he is exclusively *her* Leo and she appreciates this greatly. She has Leo buried with great pomp and circumstance and has hysterics at the funeral. Now she devotes all her time, money and energy to Leo's memory. "My Leo", if you listen to her, was the noblest creature and the most loyal and devoted husband who ever trod this earth. Abélard, compared with Leo Doros, seems to have been a fickle skirt-chaser. Philemon bilked Baucis; only Leo loved Matilda. And Leo Doros has grown in the family mythology into a great and immortal poet, too. A posthumous volume of his poetry was printed and long appreciations appeared in the Hungarian Press of America, with Leo's photograph. The estate business goes on,

you see, and advertisements are still needed. A few incorrupt-
ibles made fun of his trash but they were labelled Fascists,
Communists, liberals, anti-Semites and Jews. So, my dear
Matyas, if you want to make headway with Borsch, go and feed
a few birds in his garden and quote some of Leo's immortal
lines while doing so.'

'I'll think that over,' I promised. 'But what makes you think
in the first place that Borsch has any desire or inclination to
subsidise a small Hungarian magazine?'

'Oh, he might well be willing. First of all, he is quite a good
sort. Helpful and kind, unless you tread on his corns, then he
can turn nasty. He also stinks with money. He simply doesn't
know how to get rid of it. He is a sort of intellectual snob too,
on rather a low level. He would like to see himelf as a patron
of the arts and a man with political views of his own. Besides,
he is already doing something in this field.'

'He already supports a magazine?'

'No, of course not. But he is a patron of the sciences. Say,
good thing you brought that up, you ought to know about it.
Have you heard of Professor Hazay-Hirschfeld?'

'Never.'

'God, you don't know anyone.'

He looked at his watch but as the train was a crawler and
kept stopping every three minutes, we had time.

'Hazay-Hirschfeld was Professor of History at Szeged University. His speciality was the Thirty Years' War between 1622
and 1627. I bet he has no idea how the Thirty Years' War
started or why; I don't think he knows—or cares—how it
ended. But he knows every goddam thing that happened
between 1622 and 1627. That's what he calls specialisation.
Only amateurs dabble in whole epochs, he holds: the real
historian is always a specialist. Borsch is honoured that this
great man is his friend—and sure thing he is, he practically
lives there. He goes home only to sleep. Hazay-Hirschfeld
managed to persuade Borsch to become a patron of the sciences

and send scientific and art books to his old Alma Mater, Szeged University.'

'Well, that's jolly decent of him, after all,' I murmured. 'But why art books?'

'Because art books are very expensive. This is quite a scheme, you see. Every month Hazay-Hirschfeld hands over a carefully picked list of books to Borsch. As a rule, it's a list of the most expensive books on the market. *Gardenias*, with colour plates, 90 dollars; *The Mosques of Southern Anatolia*, 85 dollars; and stacks of tomes on electronics, or thermometer calibration, or ballistic galvanometers or the decline of the Sumerian Empire. One of Borsch's secretaries then buys these books and sends them to Professor Vadas, at Szeged. Vadas used to be Professor of Heraldry at the same university. The Communists got rid of him, partly because he refused to lick the boots of Party Secretaries and partly because they are not too keen on heraldry. As soon as the books arrive in Szeged, Vadas is informed by the customs that he has to pay a large amount of duty. He sternly refuses to pay, which means the parcels are returned unopened to Hazay-Hirschfeld, whose name figures as sender. He takes the books to a Hungarian bookseller in White Plains who buys them at half the published price—good business for all concerned. Half of the takings goes to Professor Vadas— Hazay-Hirschfeld is scrupulously honest, as you may have gathered from what I said previously—and he, of course, keeps the other half. That's how Borsch supports science in the homeland and that's how Professors Hazay-Hirschfeld and Vadas can spend their old age in reasonable comfort.'

I am not easily intimidated but, having listened to these thumbnail sketches, I approached my destination with trepidation. Sam must have guessed my thoughts.

'Don't you worry,' said Sam. 'And don't feel sorry for Borsch either. He is stinking with money.'

I fell silent. It was difficult for me to think of Borsch as a man stinking with money. My recollections of him were quite different and hard to square with this new portrait of the millionaire patron of art and science.

I remembered him as a little man with a well-trimmed red moustache, always a bit shabby, but exaggeratedly polite. He once came to see me in the boarding house in Bayswater, where I stayed in those days, to find out if there was going to be a war. I was the London correspondent of a Budapest daily and he thought, quite mistakenly, that I knew more about the future than other people.

'I am not going to take up much of your valuable time, Mr Matyas,' he smiled politely. 'I only want to know if there's going to be a war.'

'I'm afraid not,' I replied with a sigh.

This was just before the Munich agreement, in the days of Chamberlain's frantic journeyings to and fro, when we—continental journalists, émigrés, refugees, and other scum of the earth—were all afraid that Britain would settle for a compromise with the Nazis which, unless some miraculous recovery were to change matters, would mean that this country too would gradually slip into the grip, or at least under the increased influence, of the Germans. Borsch sighed with me.

'Won't there be a war at all?' he went on inquiringly. 'Not even next year? Or in 1940? Or in 1945?'

'I don't know. If they sell out Czecho-Slovakia now, they may go on selling out everybody else to save what they call peace.'

'But you will know, won't you, when war is about to break out? I mean just a day or two before?'

'Well—yes. I daresay I shall be able to foretell it a few days beforehand, whether that's *it* or just another sell-out.'

He then spoke deliberately, weighing every word carefully.

'I want you to do me a big favour, Mr Matyas. When you really feel sure that war is about to break out, let me know. Ring me up; send someone with a message. Reach me in one way or another. It is of vital importance to me. I shall reward you very liberally. In the meantime, can you lend me five shillings?'

After a little haggling, we settled for half-a-crown. However, I could not fail to point out to him the slight incongruity of his promise of a princely reward with his begging for half-crowns.

'You are quite wrong, Mr Matyas. You don't understand, if I may say so,' said Borsch with an apologetic smile. 'I was a very young man in Budapest, when the last war broke out. I was a clerk at a small engineering works. As soon as the Monarchy—as Austria-Hungary was called in those days—sent its ultimatum to Serbia, my boss, a cunning and greedy old fox, bought up all the copper cable he could lay hands on. I heard him remark that in wartime there was bound to be a shortage of copper cable and it would be worth its weight in gold. Sure enough a few months later there was a terrible shortage of copper cable and my boss became a multimillionaire. That he eventually ended up in a workhouse is quite a different story and is not strictly to the point. I learnt my lesson, Mr Matyas. I decided that if there was ever another war I, too, would buy up all the copper cable on the market.'

'Speculation is not for people like you and me, Mr Borsch,' I retorted. 'If *we* buy copper cable then, I'm sure, it'll turn out we ought to have bought something else; perhaps one ought to have *sold* copper cable. I don't really know, buying and selling is a mysterious world for me. It always works with some people; never with others.'

'I am afraid I usually belong to these others, Mr Matyas,' he replied with a wistful smile. 'But I can't go wrong this time. I have seen what I've seen. Copper cable is the secret. When there is a war, there is always a shortage of copper cable. If you let me know in time, I shall grow rich and I shall be able to pay you a princely reward—a well deserved commission. But until then I'm poor and I need five shillings from you.'

'We have agreed on half-a-crown, Mr Borsch,' I reminded him.

'Yes, I forgot,' he nodded amicably. 'But you must promise not to forget me when the time comes.'

I was in Scotland when the news of the Ribbentrop-Molotov Pact broke. It was a desperate situation to find myself out of London at such an hour. I jumped into the hired car I had with me, firmly resolved not to stop before reaching the Foreign Office building in Downing Street, where the Press conferences were held and the official spokesmen resided. Somewhere in Darlington I remembered Borsch and dashed into a post office. Unwilling to send an alarmist telegram, I wired: 'The day of copper cable is dawning.'

He bought copper cable to the value of £37,000. At first I was surprised at this sum. Little did I know about business in those days. Little did I know that to borrow five shillings was an arduous task but to get credit for £37,000 was child's play. A desperate shortage of copper cable developed in no time, and Borsch found himself quite a rich man and a few weeks later became the head of a prosperous engineering firm entrusted with valuable war contracts. Copper cable did the trick —it had been worth waiting for his chance for a quarter of a century.

The princely reward he had offered me was to have been £500, a generous reward indeed for a cable—not even a copper cable—telling him what everybody else knew in any case. I was foolish enough to refuse his offer. I remembered his words: he had called it a 'commission' and I had my idiotic prejudices. I could have accepted a gift, or a fee for my advice, but never a commission. Looking back, I fail to understand my attitude. Nowadays, whenever I have reason to be deeply ashamed of myself, I always remember that I am the man who once refused an offer of £500 and my feelings of superiority and self-respect are at once restored. I am not ashamed of having been idiotic; to accept a 'commission' would definitely have been *infra dig*.

Borsch was offended by my refusal and he kept away from me for a long time. In February 1942 I received a letter from him, written on his firm's notepaper but bearing a strange post-mark, inviting me for lunch to one of the expensive Soho restaurants. 'I know you are busy but I implore you to come,' he wrote. 'Implore' is a strong word, so I went. When I arrived, Borsch was already there, sitting at a table, in the company of a stranger.

'This is Mr Higgins.' Borsch introduced the man with obvious disgust.

It turned out that Borsch had been interned by the British authorities when Hungary became a belligerent in December 1941. His factory was under contract to the Ministry of Aircraft Production and it was the rule that one single person and one only was allowed to see the blue-prints which, when not in use, were kept locked up in the safe. Only this one chosen person was allowed to be in possession of the key to the safe. In his own firm, Borsch was this privileged individual, enjoying the full confidence of the Ministry of Aircraft Production. When he was whisked off to the Isle of Man as a dangerous enemy alien, his second-in-command—an Englishman, called Haynes— applied for the blue-prints and the key to the safe to be now transferred to his custody since it was 'not convenient that Mr Borsch should have them'. The Ministry of Aircraft Production, however, saw no inconvenience in this at all. They trusted Mr Borsch and, besides, they were only too pleased to cock a snook at the Home Office. Only one person was to see those blue-prints and that one was to remain their trusted and beloved Borsch. So Borsch—the enemy alien locked up by the Home Office—had to be brought over about once a week from the Isle of Man to handle those top-secret blue-prints which even his British-born assistant manager was not allowed to see. Borsch checked whatever required checking, saw what progress had been made in the interest of keeping the R.A.F. in the skies, doled out work for the coming week, issued all the necessary instructions and then travelled back to the Isle of Man to sojourn there as a suspected foreign spy until his services in the interest of the war effort were needed again, next week.

I found this most amusing; Borsch did not.

Mr Higgins was the detective who accompanied Borsch, and in his presence we had to speak English. But even the detective's presence did not prevent Borsch from making bitter and contemptuous attacks on the British. His feelings and pride were deeply hurt. He had been a great British patriot, in fact more than that, a preposterous Anglo-snob but internment had changed his feelings. It was not merely an injustice—which he might have tolerated as a sacrifice—but an excommunication which he could not bear. He had been told only too clearly that he did not belong.

'I used to be the most patriotic man in Britain,' he complained during lunch. 'I should have been proud to give my life for this country. And look how they treat me. It's a shame. It's disgraceful. I hate them now.'

I murmured something about the country having to be very careful and his absolute reliability would soon be re-established. He would be released in no time.

'You don't understand,' he argued fiercely. 'You have no idea how I feel. They left *you* alone. I am good enough to manufacture components for bombers but I cannot be trusted to walk around the streets.'

He threw his knife and fork down on his plate and went on angrily: 'Do you know what happened a few weeks ago? We couldn't get to sleep till 3 o'clock in the morning because of the rumpus coming from the Japanese huts. They were having a party. They had received official permission to buy champagne and stay up. Do you know *what* they were celebrating? The Japanese victory at Pearl Harbour. When we protested next day, we were told that after all Pearl Harbour *was* a great national victory for the Japanese and it would have been unfair to forbid them to celebrate just because we look at these things from a different angle. "A different angle"—that's the expression he used.'

He choked with anger.

'I was surprised to find that there were no celebrations at the fall of Singapore, a few days ago. The next thing would be to allow the Nazi internees to celebrate *their* victories. Perhaps they *did* celebrate the collapse of France and their attack on Holland and Belgium, and all their other war crimes. I don't know, I wasn't in yet—and why not let them have a champagne party on Hitler's birthday? Just because we look at Hitler from a different angle?'

He drew breath and continued with deliberation: 'I hate the British now. This war will be over one day and we . . . I mean, the English and their allies, will win it, in spite of such fools who lock me up while they permit the Japs to celebrate Allied defeats. When this war is over I'll go to America. I don't like the idea but I'll go. I'll come back only once in a while, just on an occasional visit.'

Mr Higgins took no part in the conversation. At first, when we were discussing the weather and the regrettable shortage of sherry, he was pleasant and amiable enough. But now, while Borsch was raving against his country, he sat there with an inscrutable glare, as if he understood nothing.

'And now I'm going to spend a penny,' said Borsch and stood up. 'Excuse me.'

The detective stood up, too.

'And so am I,' said Higgins. 'I know, of course, that you're not going to do a bunk, Mr Borsch. You wouldn't let me down, would you? All the same, it's better to be on the safe side.'

That was the last straw for Borsch. He came back to the table and, red in the face, shouted: 'No! Not even for visits. I shan't come back at all. Never.'

And, with a great deal of dignity, he walked into the lavatory followed closely by Higgins.

Borsch's idea in inviting me for lunch was to discuss with me what I could do to help along his release. I did what I could; on one occasion I even paid a short visit to the camp. His anti-British fulminations must have delayed his release by six months at least. Eventually, however, just before Christmas 1942, he was set free. He was convinced that I had played a major part

33

in achieving his release which was nonsense. As soon as he was out, he wanted to see me and thank me and probably give me something. But I was too busy in those days and tired of his anti-British ravings. So I did not meet him and, in fact, never saw him again after saying goodbye to him in the Isle of Man, in the most depressing circumstances.

He was as good as his word. As soon as the war was over he sold his house, transferred his very considerable assets and moved to the United States. He was deeply hurt and now hated the English almost as much as he had once loved them.

SAM'S SECRET

'Hiya,' said Borsch in the truest American fashion when he spotted us among the twenty-five or thirty people who got out at Port Washington.

'Nice to see you,' said I. 'You haven't changed a bit.'

I should probably have said that even if I had found him scarcely recognisable but the truth was that he looked surprisingly young. His red moustache had turned greyish and his hair, although arranged and distributed with meticulous and loving care, had obviously thinned; still, on the whole, he looked remarkably well preserved. I made some quick calculations, remembering that he had his first job—he was just a lad then—when World War I broke out, and decided that now, in 1955, he must be about fifty-seven or fifty-eight. He was wearing flannels and tweed jacket and looked so British that the Duke of Windsor would have seemed a Central European refugee next to him.

'What's new in the homeland?' he asked.

That was a tricky question. Of course, Hungary was our common homeland; I also knew that he had left England in a huff never to return, yet, looking at his ultra-British attire, I felt certain that he had Britain in mind. He was an obvious victim of the bug of Anglomania, pretty widespread in the United States in those days. Most people in America would willingly have given huge sums to acquire Anglo-Saxon ancestors; many of them *did*, in fact, give huge sums. There was a brisk trade in Anglo-Saxon forebears and really good forefathers were not at all cheap. Borsch, of course, could afford not only respectable Midland traders or devout Puritans who fled to the New World to keep the flag of freedom flying but—had he fancied—even some obscure Scottish earl. But he was a man of taste and moderation. He realised that he was too recent an arrival in the United States and he was fully aware that his strong Anglo-Hungarian accent would hardly fit in with the fiction of descent from a long line of Dukes of Ross and Cromarty. So, with admirable restraint and with some ingenuity, he had decided to be his own Anglo-Saxon ancestry. After all, we lived in an era of do-it-yourself.

I gave him the latest news from the homeland. I told him whatever I could remember of what Princess Margaret and the Queen Mother were doing; I informed him that Cambridge had won the Boat Race by sixteen lengths; I told him—to cheer him up—that his old football team, Arsenal, looked like winning the Cup (which they did not proceed to do); and I added that his old friend, Sandor Balogh, who had become a pig-iron-millionaire in England, was desperately angling for a knighthood by supporting many more or less respectable charities but so far had only managed a miserable O.B.E. This last bit of news pleased him immensely and he laughed aloud at Balogh's vanity.

'Ridiculous things, titles,' he said with the superiority of a man who would die to get one.

Sam agreed that they were.

'You there, Jim?'

This question was addressed to a chauffeur, wearing the customary dark-blue uniform and peaked cap of the English chauffeur who, with superior and inscrutable demeanour, awaits his master in a huge Rolls in front of the London Ritz (and since the car cost £10,000 or more, the police act as though it were not obstructing the road). Jim stepped forward and said:

'Yes.'

Now, *yes* is a simple little word, rather a short one, containing none of the pitfalls of English pronunciation: no *th*-s; no *r*-s; no treacherous *l*-s. *Yes*, one would have thought, was one of the most innocuous words in the English tongue. Yet, when Jim uttered this *yes*, I immediately knew not only that he was a

36

Hungarian but also that he had come from Transdanubia—in fact, from the neighbourhood of Szombathely.

'You know, Mr Borsch . . .' Sam was starting to say in the car, when Borsch interrupted him:

'Cut out the "Mr". No need to be formal. Just call me I.V. All big bosses . . . well, people who have risen to some position in life, I mean . . . are called nowadays by their first two initials.'

'I know the I is for Ivan,' I remarked. 'What does the V stand for?'

'Nothing. Sorry about that. I have only one Christian name. My parents, in Hungary, were very poor. They couldn't afford two Christian names. It's a ridiculous handicap in this country. I got the V as a personal gift from P.T. My friend, you know, P. T. Trotter, President of the local Republicans, a very substantial realtor. He started calling me I.V. and now everybody does.'

His friend, P.T. was mentioned four more times during the short journey between the station and Borsch's house. The house itself was superb, a splendid mansion in imitation colonial style. We saw, as Jim drove in under the huge trees, that it stood right on the sea-shore, with its own beach and sheds for motor boats. We passed a large fountain with a nude shepherd boy, blowing a flute.

On arrival, Borsch introduced us to Mrs Doros, the tycoon-poet's widow, a tiny, shrunken, dry and disagreeable woman with small pig-eyes and prickly manners. Sam greeted her with an exaggerated courtesy and warmth which was received with an icy snub. Borsch gave us whiskies and chatted a few minutes on various subjects, but mostly on P. T. Trotter, a great friend of his, a very substantial realtor and President of the local Republicans. Then Hazay-Hirschfeld, the old professor, turned up and Borsch told him to show us round.

'If you look forward to seeing a monument of bad taste,' the Professor began his guided tour, 'you will be a little disappointed. It's bad enough, of course, but it could be much worse. Borsch—I must call him I.V., which is too bad—well, Borsch is after all a European, and no European can sink to the depths a true-born American can at times. There are only two real abominations in the whole house. Two major ones, I mean. Number One is here, on the left, a Chinese room. I.V. has filled it with all things Chinese—or rather with all the things people managed to sell him as Chinese. Junk bought from shady New York antique dealers—oriental furniture, carpets, opium pipes. Look at this porcelain elephant, made in Frankfurt. Or this small bamboo pagoda. Not bad for Manchester. There are some Japanese oddments and Malayan bric-à-brac. Well, near enough. I mean Japan and Malaya are near enough to China— so we won't quarrel with minute details. A few Javanese heads and Bali skirts—on the wall, up there—have been thrown in, for good measure. I don't know why he wanted a Chinese room at all. Or maybe I do. Perhaps he has set his heart on seeming exotic; in order to prevent people from noticing how exotic he looks in any case. He is desperately trying to be what he cannot help being anyway. Human nature, you know.'

I could see Sam was enjoying the Professor's lecture as much as I was.

'And this is the second major abomination. A faithful copy of the Café Calabria from Budapest, once many years ago his favourite camping place. Borsch loves America and condones all the horror and depravity of what he likes to call the American Way of Life but which Henry Miller, I think more appropriately, called the Air-Conditioned Nightmare. However, even Borsch deplores the lack of Budapest coffee-houses in this country. That the same coffee-houses are, by now, extinct in Budapest, too, doesn't matter in the least. They exist in his memory and one's memory is the only reality. Anyway, he deprecates the absence of coffee-houses in his blessed U.S., so he set out to remedy this flaw and had one built. Look at the marble tables; the hideous candelabra; the gloomy provincial elegance of those red plush chairs, recalling a place called

Kaposvar in 1852, but all made according to careful and extremely expensive designs in New York, in A.D. 1952. Every morning, American and Hungarian newspapers are put into those ridiculous bamboo frames which went out of fashion even in the Hungarian provinces twenty years ago. He had them made in New York. Notice the cashier's box in the middle; that's where the cashier girl, a semi-official prostitute (always peroxide blonde) used to sit in the old days, diffusing her often fading charms. Borsch, at parties, makes one of his lady guests occupy that box and all women regard it as a place of honour.'

The Professor's eye wandered over the café with disgust.

'In the old days,' he added, 'every provincial coffee-house went to great expense to turn itself into a "home"; I.V.'s boast is that he has managed to turn his home into a provincial coffee-house.'

Borsch passed in the corridor behind us.

'Are you explaining everything to the gentlemen?' he asked Hazay-Hirschfeld.

'*Everything*,' replied the Professor with sinister emphasis.

'Do they like it?'

'They are overwhelmed,' said Hazay-Hirschfeld fruitfully.

'The rest is not bad,' he told us, walking on as soon as Borsch had gone. 'It's mostly English style. In fact, a bit of a mixture of styles and periods, but never mind. He has some Chippendale furniture and two Whistlers and a Graham Sutherland. All very English. The homeland, you know. He would like his parents' bones to rest in English soil. I shouldn't be surprised if one day he has them exhumed in Miskolc and reburied at Leeds.'

We walked across the garden to see the motor launches in their hangar. The garden was a beautifully kept park of vast dimensions, with a tennis court, putting green, and the fountain with the nude shepherd boy playing his flute. Two Hungarian peasants—a man and a woman—dressed as respectable Negro servants from Alabama, passed and greeted us in a rich, broad Southern drawl. I mean the rich drawl of Southern Hungary.

'The gardener and his wife. She's the cook,' the Professor explained.

'Look here,' I said to the Professor, 'are there any Americans around here at all?'

'Americans?' He repeated the word with great surprise in his voice.

'Americans?' exclaimed Sam, too, as if he had heard the word for the first time.

'My dear Matyas,' said the Professor solemnly, 'I doubt if Borsch even knows any Americans. I'm sure he has seen some, but I doubt if he has spoken to many. Nor have I, for that matter. Well, there are a few exceptions, prize specimens, such as P.T., the substantial realtor, President of the local Republicans. I am astonished that an old émigré like yourself should ask such a naïve question. Maybe it's different in Britain; I wouldn't know. But here, my dear Matyas, Americans are purely peripheral in our lives. We live in ghettoes. In business life I.V. meets an occasional American here and there; he can't help dealing with Americans—although they often turn out to be Mexicans, Bolivians, Italians and Germans. He also employs Americans—every office, I am told, needs one or two people who can speak the language of the land without doing violence to every sentence and debasing every word. But these Americans are not really part of life; they belong to the scenery, like the bay over there or the Empire State Building; they are not essential parts of real life. We only meet Hungarians. Or ex-Hungarians. In the best case, people of Hungarian origin. In the very best case: American wives of people of Hungarian origin. But they are the limit.'

We were now walking back towards the house.

'New York may be a vast American metropolis for most people,' the Professor continued, 'but for us it is a small Hungarian village. Or rather a middle-sized Hungarian town, with its own dignitaries, its own special snobberies, its own Press, its own gossip and jealousies, crimes, jokes and tragedies. America is only the background to this life: its venue, that's

all. Our life is inside America only in the sense that a small con-
centric circle is inside a bigger circle: we copy the Americans,
we take over their habits; we go to their super-markets; we
buy their products and drive on their super highways; we
imitate their manners, we buy new outfits at Easter and eat
turkey on Thanksgiving Day. In some ways we are much more
American than the Americans but it is only our children—if
any—who will be real Americans and become integral parts
of the air-conditioned nightmare. We all look forward to this
with pride but we, ourselves, go on living in our ghettoes. And
mind you: *they* didn't lock us up in those ghettoes: *we* locked
ourselves up. And we defend the walls from within—as in the
long run the walls of all ghettoes are always defended. A ghetto
is a warm, friendly place; the outside world is hostile and, as
we have said, pretty nightmarish.'

'Does Borsch suffer because of this?' Sam asked thoughtfully.

'Not consciously,' the Professor replied. 'He suffers to some
extent because all his life he has been an outsider; he was always
out in the dark, trying to get in; and whether he was trying to
invade the circle of the rich, or the circle of the English, or
the Americans, or the Republicans, they always allowed him a
peep but never let him in. He negotiated all the barriers,
breached the walls, crossed the Rubicons—yet, somehow, he
managed to remain the eternal outsider. But he doesn't realise
this and he doesn't suffer consciously. He thinks he is in. He
doesn't know that it was easy to emigrate from Budapest to
London; that it was child's play to emigrate from London to
New York; but that no matter how many years he spends here
and no matter how hard he tries: to emigrate from New York
into America is impossible for him.

'That explains, at least partially, the Chinese room and the
Café Calabria,' the Professor added as we were entering the
house. 'It's a pity that almost all fascinating human problems
end up in such monstrosities, but I cannot help it. And even if
I could, I wouldn't. I do not wish to change the world. Not any
more.'

I don't want to sound boastful but I believe that both Sam and I handled our errand in masterly fashion. Nevertheless, although Borsch sounded sympathetic and interested from the outset, he did not let himself be carried away by our performance. He remained sympathetic and interested throughout, but we failed to kindle the flames of wild enthusiasm.

We settled round the little marble tables of the Café Calabria. The gardener, dressed in the garb of an Austro-Hungarian head waiter of the eighteen-nineties—tails and black tie—served us gin and tonic, and whisky and soda (no dry Martinis, no Tom Collinses, no Bourbon on the rocks in this house; even the whiskey was not referred to as *Scotch*, and you could have it *neat* but not *straight*). The gardener's wife sat in the cashier's box, doing nothing in particular. We duly admired everything and exclaimed several times: 'How original!' When, at last, we all settled down to listen to Sam's exposé, Mrs Doros—before Sam could open his mouth—remarked dryly: 'You want money, I bet.'

'Well,' said Sam as diplomatically as he could, 'it is not quite as simple as that.'

'It's never very simple,' the shrunken little lady replied acidly, 'but in the end it all boils down to a request for cash.'

'Let Mr MacKay speak, Matilda,' Borsch reprimanded her.

'They always come for money,' Mrs Doros said again, just to make her point clear, in case anyone had found her previous remarks too subtle.

Looking at the little witch, I decided she must be won over. The scheme was doomed to failure unless Mrs Doros was on our side.

Sam proceeded with his exposé: he was shrewd, tactful and sounded very sensible. He acknowledged Borsch's past generosity and underlined the tremendous—he did not go so far as to say world-shaking—importance of this scheme.

'I.V. is already doing a great deal,' Hazay-Hirschfeld remarked. 'I don't know if you have heard of his magnificent efforts in sending scientific works to Szeged University?'

'We do know *all* about that,' Sam replied and I thought his answer sounded like a veiled threat. But then he added in a different tone:

'We do appreciate his efforts; and we do appreciate yours, too, Professor. Our own work will not be confined to publishing the magazine. That's our main scheme, of course, but we have other plans in mind. One of them is a vast expansion of the book scheme.'

Borsch's face darkened on hearing this, so Sam hastened to add: 'What I mean is this: we mean a modest expansion of the scheme. But we shall spare no effort . . .'

I feared he would speak of no stones to be left unturned and no avenues left unexplored. But he did not forget himself to quite such an extent.

'The book scheme,' he said and his brow perspired, 'is an important activity and we wish to see it grow. And I hope we may count on your continued help, Professor. We should like to leave this matter in your experienced hands.'

The Professsor blinked. Now he, in turn, sounded somewhat menacing when he assured us that indeed we could count on his continued help. His experienced hands would go on doing the same as before and if he was to get more books, he was, heart and soul, for this venture, devoted servant of science that he was.

Sam's shameless bribery of the Professor in public, gave me the idea of perverting Mrs Doros just as brazenly.

'Sam and I,' I said, 'have yet another pet idea and I wonder if we could gain your approval, Mrs Doros. It is essential.'

'You gotta hope,' she replied. 'What is it?'

'I believe that your late husband, Leo Doros, is greatly underrated as a poet.'

She looked at me and replied, her voice still edged with hostility: 'He had too many enemies.'

'Perhaps because he was at the same time a successful busi-
nessman and people still cling to the idea that a truly great poet
must starve in a garret. That's why people try to belittle
him.'

'To *forget* him,' she corrected sharply. 'To eradicate him
from the pages of world literature.'

'Quite,' I replied with a straight face. 'And that is a grave
injustice. We have decided—Sam and I—that our magazine will
put that right. We are going to encourage the writing of good
poetry. . . .'

All this was news to Sam but he cottoned on fast enough.

' . . . Encourage the writing of good poetry, mostly in Leo's
style—about the suffering of birds and suchlike,' said Sam, a
shade too obviously; but, I felt, the 'suchlike' had put it right,
somehow.

Borsch looked worried: I knew he was working out what it
would cost him. But we gave him no chance of butting in.

'Yes,' I nodded grimly, and then added with due emphasis,
'once a year we are going to award a Leo Doros Prize.'

'Someone will hand it over,' said Sam, none too subtly but
significantly. And Mrs Doros did not miss the point.

'This is not so simple as you seem to think, gentlemen,' she
retorted. 'It will have to be discussed in great detail before I
can give my consent.'

But this was only her natural inclination to remain difficult
and tiresome. We knew that the idea of the Leo Doros Prize
was a winner.

Sam went on talking of other matters, Danubian unity and
whether the Poles could be included or not. Everything seemed
to be flowing smoothly now, but Borsch was not forthcoming
enough. Whatever else he may have been, we had never thought
of him as stingy and close-fisted—but that was what he was
proving to be. We were prepared for an outright refusal;
but not for this careful weighing up of every cent.

'How much money would you need, you said?' he asked.

'Three hundred.'

'Well, I have to discuss that with the others.'

'Three hundred is not such a lot of money,' Sam retorted rather peevishly.

'I never said it was,' Borsch replied good-naturedly. 'But I must discuss it with my friends. We've been talking over these problems for some time and I can't go along on my own. Besides, I need their financial help, too.'

'Their financial help?' I repeated incredulously.

'We're about ten of us,' Borsch continued, 'or even more. If we decide to launch this scheme—and I don't say yes or no at the moment—but if we decide to launch it, we'll all want to contribute.'

'About two dollars fifty per head,' I thought but said nothing.

'It's not a large sum,' he smiled apologetically as if he had guessed my thoughts. 'I never said it was. But it needs a certain amount of consideration and planning all the same— political as well as financial. Sam, can I have your plan in writing? Not the budget—we shall have to go into that on our own—just the ideas.'

'Yes, you can.'

'When?'

'Now,' said Sam producing a memorandum from the inside pocket of his jacket. I did not know he had one prepared; but he knew the way things were done here.

'Fine,' said Borsch, handing it to the gardener's wife. 'Go and put that on my desk, my dear.'

The girl disappeared, then Borsch turned to me:

'How long are you staying?'

I told him that I meant to return to London at the end of the coming week but had not yet decided on the day.

Borsch left the room and we heard the telephone tinkling. He came back after a few minutes.

'I've just had a word with P.T.–P.T. Trotter, you know, a substantial realtor. President of the local Republicans. A great friend of mine. You come out here next Thursday and we'll all

45

meet at his house. The others will be there, too. And now let's go and eat something.'

We did not know whether to be pleased or disappointed. But the idea of food was welcome so I stood up eagerly.

'His lawyer will also come along,' Borsch added.

'His lawyer?' Sam asked. He sounded flabbergasted.

'And my lawyer. And perhaps another lawyer or two.'

We sighed and knew that all the lawyers would get *their* three hundred; but what about ours?

3

The serious complication started during the fork-supper. After a drink or two in the other room, we returned to the Café Calabria and our hearts sprang up with joy. Borsch may have been an Anglo-snob but, in the field of gastronomics, he had enough sense to remain an ardent Hungarian patriot. There were many kinds of cold sausage and what the Americans call cold cuts: all specially made by a Hungarian butcher in the Bronx. On huge, blue Wedgwood dishes we had four types of ham—some smoked, some cooked—and one whole enormous peasant-ham among them. There was smoked goose-breast as well as cold chicken, cold turkey, cold goose and a dozen partridges. At the other end of the long table—made up of four or five little marble coffee-house tables pushed together— four different salads smiled at us most invitingly: herring salad, Russian salad, tomato salad and cucumber salad. There was a vast dish with a *fogas*—it weighed seventeen pounds, as I was to find out later. This celebrated white fish of Lake Balaton had been flown over from Hungary and was served with tartar and béchamel sauces, both produced with loving care and endless labour. I just did not know what to choose. I knew that having selected the most marvellous dish, I would discover something even better, and would only regret that—try as I might—I could eat no more as, alas, there is a limit to everything.

Before deciding, I looked at the wines. There were some magnificent Hungarian white wines, one bearing the impressive name of *Debröi Hárslevelü*, the other the equally formidable name of *Badacsonyi Kéknyelü:* no sweet and overpraised Tokay wines here. For more cosmopolitan tastes a white *Chateauneuf de Pape* was served (the red is a famous wine; I was proud that Borsch knew and appreciated the white variety) and there was also champagne for the enjoyment of the ignorant and the snob.

Sam was filling his plate with great care, deliberation and moderation. Suddenly his hand stopped in mid-air, his eyes goggled and became riveted on a dish well to the back of the buffet-table. Following his bewitched and reverent glance I almost went down on my knees myself: there was a huge goose-liver. This dish is practically unknown in England where geese must not be forcibly fed—for that great delicacy is, in fact, a diseased liver. I had thought that goose-livers were also unknown in the United States. Perhaps they are—I never found out. Perhaps Borsch had that flown over, too, like the Balaton fish. The main thing was that the goose-liver was here. It looked lovely, inviting and irresistible—even beautiful and elegant on its red and gold dish. Sam and the goose-liver looked at each other with the breathless tension of a Hitchcock scene. Then Sam turned his head away and walked away from the table with brisk and determined steps.

I was impressed by Sam's strength of character. Goose-liver is about the most fattening food in the world and I, too, had to think of my lines. So I helped myself to the white Balaton fish with the green sauce; having dealt with that I came back to the table for a partridge, some peasant-ham and three kinds of salad. I went back to steal another admiring and covetous look at the goose-liver—I think I also sighed—and walked away feeling holier than anyone else in the universe and sure that the virtue of self-denial ought to be renamed after me.

But, alas, I am a very weak character. My virtues are not

47

really to write home about. The image of that beautiful, undefiled goose-liver haunted me: and when Mrs Doros walked up to me with plate in hand and said that we must distribute the Prize exactly as her late, beloved, husband would have done, and I replied that all would be done in the spirit of the deceased—my mind was not really on Leo.

'With the utmost purity and integrity . . .' she said sternly.

The words 'purity' and 'integrity' conjured up the picture of Leo's dead body lying on the lift-girl in a hotel room, in Atlantic City, but even this fascinating image could not hold my attention. The goose-liver won hands down, if this be the right metaphor.

I left the Great Widow and trotted back to the buffet-table, only to receive a terrible shock. The goose-liver was not there! Not a sign of it; not a scrap of it. The whole beautiful liver was gone.

'Sam,' flashed through my brain. 'It can only be Sam.' My eyes searched for him. He was sitting at one of the hideous little marble tables, with an empty Rosenthal plate in front of him. He was still holding a knife and fork in a most ungainly fashion—quite unlike him. He stared at his empty plate with glassy eyes. Suddenly the knife fell from his hand, dropping on the valuable plate which broke into two halves. He dropped his fork, too—it seemed to me he threw it down deliberately. One of the halves of the plate broke into six or seven fragments.

Conversation died down and all eyes turned to Sam. There was deathly silence for a few seemingly endless moments. But Sam did not seem to be aware of the outside world. He went on gazing at the broken pieces of china; he was breathing heavily. At last, he kicked the chair from under him, jumped up and ran out of the room.

Borsch started chatting again, in a leisurely, conversational tone as if nothing had happened. I did not catch a single word he said although, I believe, his remarks were addressed to me.

I got up and followed Sam. I found him at the fountain, now lit by suggestive pink and green lights. He was looking the naked shepherd boy in the eyes, as if able to hear the enchanting mute strains of the flute. He took no notice of me.

After a long silence he said at last: 'I knew it was coming. I've felt it for some time.'

I still said nothing.

'I am slowly becoming the slave of a mortal passion.'

This phrase from Victorian melodrama sounded strange from his mouth. He, too, must have realised this because he gave a tired, self-conscious smile.

'It may sound odd but I feel it coming. A mortal passion. A curse.'

'What *are* you talking about, Sam?'

He fell silent again, watched the face of the shepherd boy and still listening to his music, intently.

'Do you drink?' I asked him.

He gave no reply.

He had certainly never given me the slightest impression of being an habitual drinker, let alone a drunkard. I looked at him carefully again. He was plump but not fat; his friendly blue eyes shone clearly, even now; he had an almost rosy complexion—slightly ridiculous for a man of forty-one. His mind was quick, his temper even and he always seemed contented, even gay.

'I don't believe you,' I said, although he had not really pleaded guilty to my charge. 'I don't believe you. You don't drink.'

'No,' he said at last. 'I don't drink. I eat.'

The obvious uttered with such gravity sounded comical.

'Well, we all eat,' I told him. 'We should hardly survive without food.'

'Sure,' Sam nodded grimly. 'It's true: we all eat. But we all drink, too, don't we? We should hardly survive without water or other liquids either. All the same, we all know what we mean when we say that a man drinks. My trouble is that I have started eating the way many others drink.'

He offered me a cigarette and lit one for himself.

'Tonight I realised for certain. But I've suspected it for months. Some people are drunkards; I am becoming an eatard.'

With his pleasant, slightly self-conscious smile, he added: 'That may be just a silly pun to you. To me it is a matter of life and death. It may well be the end of me.'

I suddenly remembered the three dozen oysters at the railway bar; and the way he had doodled chicken legs and breasts in a wave of nostalgia. And now the goose-liver. I still felt a pang of jealousy when I recalled it in all its glory. This man must have devoured that enormous liver on top of a huge supper. No snack to be sure; but why should it be 'the end of me'?

'Surely, Sam,' I told him, 'even if your appetite is a little heartier than most people's, this is not such a very tragic passion.'

'That's what you think. People, of course, laugh at a man who eats too much. But people laugh at all sorts of serious things.'

'That's true,' I agreed. 'I get the hiccups every now and then. People laugh at that too. It's undignified. A man who *is* hiccuping seems ridiculous to a man who isn't. I am inclined to laugh at it myself. But after three hours of violent hiccuping I cease to be amused. And after eight hours I've positively had all the fun I need for one day.'

'Mine is a mortal passion,' he repeated stubbornly. 'I know it is. Believe me,' he added, 'it is much more dreadful to get drunk on steaks, or oysters or goose-liver than on dry Martinis.'

'Come back to the house,' I suggested. 'They must be wondering what has happened to you.'

He paid no attention to this.

'I know that psycho-analysts would find an excellent if

somewhat obscure explanation for this. I could go to a psycho-analyst and, after he'd driven me crazy for four years, he'd come up with some most convincing theory. Perhaps my mother kept taking her breast away from me and now I take all the food I can lay my hands on so as to make up for the disappointment, frustration and despair—or simply for the lack of nourishment—of those early days. Maybe. And what if I do?'

'You know very well what if you do. . . .'

He went on:

'There are hundreds of possible explanations, some more complicated than others. I remember I once bought a book on popular psychology for an air journey, that had a bit in it about a girl who ate too much. I never thought that her problem might be mine one day—or perhaps I did suspect it, because the story stuck in my mind though I've forgotten all the other cases. You know what her analyst found? She was secretly and sub-consciously in love with her father and hoped—subconsciously, of course—to become pregnant by him. Filling herself up with food was supposed to be a substitute for filling her inside with her old man's baby. Does that sound convincing to you?'

'Not in your case, I'm afraid.'

'In my case, I suppose, we ought to hot it up a bit. Let's say I am a secret homosexual—even *I* don't know—secretly in love with my father (he died before the war) and my sub-sub-conscious wish is to be a woman so's he can get me in the family way. O.K. Extremely likely. But where does such an explana-tion lead to?'

'It's no good making fun of Uncle Sigmund in such a silly fashion.'

We had talked about Freud before and it was he who kept referring to the great man as Uncle Sigmund.

'There's no need to defend Uncle Sigmund against *me*. He has no greater admirer. He was a genius of the first order; for me he is also utterly useless. I used to think that he was marvellous—a kind of Copernicus of the mind—as far as our insight and self-knowledge were concerned but not very good in therapy. Those ridiculous cures, often going on for years and so often bungled by incompetent analysts—most of them unbalanced neurotics themselves, more in need of a cure than any of their patients . . . Today I'm inclined to believe that it is the other way round: psycho-analysis is most effective as a cure in cases of claustrophobia, anxiety neurosis, compulsion neurosis, agoraphobia and troubles like that, but what can it predict about ourselves? Nothing. A man suffers a terrible shock or some great indignity in early life and as a result he may become a criminal *or* a philanthropist, a sadist *or* a great surgeon, a pathological liar *or* a great poet and story-teller, a lunatic spendthrift *or* a benefactor of mankind. But which? No one can say. Very well, you may say that foreknowledge is no real knowledge. Then the analyst meets a patient—let's say with a pathological love for food—he has to find out the reasons for *his* trouble and cure him. But this is not so simple in my case. Apart from having this particular trouble, I am a completely normal, balanced, happy man. You may put it this way, if you insist; that apart from being slightly mad, I am absolutely normal. Few people can claim even that. Prolonged psycho-analytical treatment may drive me half-mad without curing my original troubles. A lot of wise things have been said about psycho-analysis but the wisest of all was the quip that psycho-analysis is really the disease it pretends to cure. No, no, my dear Matyas, I shall have to work this out for myself. I shall have to find my own remedies—perhaps with will-power, or call it what you like. I have to face those shadows: the shadows of steaks and goose-liver, the ghosts of turkeys and oxen.'

He was talking only half-seriously now, so I suggested again that we should return to the house. His absence might endanger his scheme, the success of which was so near to his heart.

He sighed.

'Go back where? To the Café Calabria, which in any normal house would be the dining-room. That's my destiny: all ways lead to the dining-room. I can see the writing on the wall: it's all written in blood. The blood of calves, sheep and chickens. Or is it my own? Never mind. Back to the Café Calabria!'

LOVE AND MONEY

Next morning a small parcel was delivered to me in my hotel room. It contained three books. One was a thin paper-back, *Christmas Carols, Religious and Secular*; the second a heavy tome: *Texan Slang and Usage*, and the third *The Virtuous Life: A Handbook for Christians*, by Canon Augustus D. Hufnagel. An accompanying slip told me that the books had been sent with the compliments of Allyears and with the best wishes of Miss Eleanor Sputz, but it contained no further information. This was a pity because I was most anxious to know why they should send me any books at all and if they did, why these three? Who had made the selection, on what basis, and what exactly had the selector got in mind—if *mind* be the right word for it? All this, however, has remained, to this day, one of the unsolved riddles of my life.

This happened on Saturday morning. I asked the travel bureau in the hotel to book me an air passage to London for Friday next. In the remaining six days I paid two memorable visits: one on Sunday to Mrs Markos, and the other on Thursday, the eve of my departure, to Mr P. T. Trotter, to hear the great decision. The first of these visits was to be a normal social occasion; both turned out a shade more eventful and dramatic than I had anticipated. And the two together changed Sam's life.

2

'Are you free on Sunday evening?' Sam asked me. 'I've got a dinner invitation for you to the Markoses.'

'Yes, I'm free. But who are the Markoses?'

'Two ladies I know. Mother and daughter.'

This sounded extremely cagey from Sam who, on such occasions, was fond of relating everything he knew about people's background, life-story and character.

'Come on,' I nudged him. 'There's more to it than that.'

'Yes, there is more to it. There is Mariska. Their maid. Miss Markos brought her out from Hungary. She's the best cook I've ever come across. She's an artist. A goddess. She'll be my undoing.'

'Why do you go to them if she'll be your undoing?'

'What a silly question. Because of that. Because she will be my undoing. We never try to avoid our fate. We always run ahead to meet it halfway. Uncle Sigmund talked to us about the death-wish. He never said a word about the plum-dumpling wish. It is also vitally important. In my case the two are identical. And I don't care. There is no better life than eating Mariska's plum-dumpling, there could be no better death than succumbing to it.'

His description took on a rhapsodical note:

'There are many people who can cook; there are many people even who can cook well. But Mariska is a genius. Mariska is a poetess. I adore Keats. Immediately after Keats comes Mariska. The "Ode on a Grecian Urn" is matched only by Mariska's plum-dumplings; the supremacy of the "Ode to a Nightingale" is only threatened by Mariska's Dobos cake.'

He stopped for a moment, then added contemptuously: 'Shelley and Eliot are just nowhere.'

'Well, that's Mariska,' said I. 'And what about the two Markos ladies?'

Sam became reticent and non-committal again: 'They are two old friends of mine. I've known them for some time.'

I felt strongly that thereby hung a tale, but I am not very inquisitive by nature so I did not press him. I always—well, in most cases—listen with interest to people if they want to tell me something. When I was younger, I found personal confessions exciting, almost intoxicating. In fact I knew no greater

55

excitement than communion between two souls, however commonplace and uninteresting the souls involved may have been. But becoming a trifle middle-aged, I began to find such communications and self-revelations tiresome and embarrassing. I liked Sam but I left it to him to tell me as much of his affairs as he thought fit.

He said unexpectedly: 'As I have told you about my real problems, there is no reason why I shouldn't tell you about my sex-life, too. It's pretty public, after all.'

I listened with increasing interest. But he remained silent. Having announced the revelations to come, he kept them to himself. I was still unenlightened as to the state of things when we rang the bell of the Markos ladies' apartment.

The door was opened by a healthy, pretty peasant woman in her mid-thirties. She had an apple-red face of vaguely Slavonic cast, with high cheekbones; she was wearing a multi-coloured headscarf, tied behind her ears, as is the custom in certain districts of Transdanubia.

'This is Mariska,' Sam introduced her. 'She is an admirable woman. Easily the greatest cook in the world.'

Mariska smiled with delight.

'Oh, Mr MacKay . . .' (she pronounced the name in its Hungaro-Scottish version) 'you speak as if I were the Eisenhover.'

I was not pained by the mispronunciation of the President's name, but I was surprised to hear that he, too, ranked among the world's greatest cooks.

'What's news, Mariska?' asked Sam.

'Plum-dumplings tonight.'

Sam knelt down and kissed her hand.

'I'm not the Eisenhover . . .' she protested, laughing.

'Do you like it here, Mariska?' I asked her, trying to make polite conversation.

'New York . . .' (she pronounced it Nave-York) 'is all right; Kis-Harsany was all right, too. What's the difference?'

I did not quite feel up to explaining then and there the difference between New York and the village of Kis-Harsany. But, on second thoughts, perhaps she had a point there: the inside of a saucepan looks very much alike in both places; and I felt it was doubtful whether she had seen much else in either place.

'You aren't homesick?'

'What for should I be homesick?' she answered pleasantly. 'When I'm here I can't be there.'

'I never said she was a great intellect,' Sam remarked when we sat down in the drawing-room to await the two ladies. 'She's no egghead. Pascal was wittier; Aldous Huxley's knowledge is wider; F. R. Leavis is more widely read; William James was a more original thinker. But she *is* the best cook in the world.'

'Your two lady-friends must be very rich to afford a maid,' I told him. 'I've always heard that to have a maid in America is the pinnacle of luxury.'

'It is, but Mariska is no ordinary case. Martha—Miss Markos —was born and lived in Kis-Harsany but was determined to come to New York where they had some relations and, also a job, for the asking. Her parents were dead against such a plan, particularly as the outlook in those days—immediately after the war—was fairly rosy in Hungary. But Martha was adamant—she always is, in everything—and in the end her parents agreed, on condition that she took Mariska with her. Mariska's mother had served Martha's grandparents (the family had a timber yard), and Mariska, too, had been with the family since she reached the age of twelve. So Martha, who was seventeen in 1946, left Kis-Harsany for New York, in Mariska's company. Six years later Markos—a completely ruined, jobless man and a nervous wreck by then—died, and Martha asked her mother to join her in the United States. Conditions had gone from bad to worse in Hungary and even to apply for an American visa under the Rakosi terror was a heinous crime, something akin to high treason. But, after

Stalin's death when the first thaw came, Elza Markos managed to obtain a visa and—more difficult in her case—a Hungarian passport, and arrived here not very long ago. As for them being millionaires . . . no, they are not. Mariska's wages have sometimes been left unpaid in the past. When she is paid, it is a pittance compared with American wages; but, no doubt, it's a fabulous sum compared with what she'd get in Kis-Harsany.'

Miss Martha Markos appeared and I found her manners a little sharp and prickly. She was neither pretty nor unattractive but her face did not appeal to me.

'My mother won't be a minute. She's just finishing her face. It takes longer and longer, I'm afraid.'

The mother did not labour in vain. As her daughter was now twenty-six, she could not be much younger than forty-six—but she looked about thirty-five—and a charming, girlish thirty-five at that.

'Mother has to spend quite a little bit of her time in front of the mirror nowadays,' said Martha cattishly, in front of her mother.

'Alas, I'm getting on. We can't all be as young and lovely as you are, my dear.' This rejoinder, delivered by the charming mother to her daughter—no beauty queen by any standards —sounded like biting sarcasm; but looking at Elza's frank open face and her innocent smile, I was inclined to believe that it was meant, in fact, as a compliment.

The dinner started with *goulash* and the appearance of that dish recalled long-forgotten rituals of my childhood. When we were children we—my sister, my brother and I—used to spend every summer in Transylvania, with our uncle and aunt who had three boys. Plum-dumpling days were special occasions, high-lights of our holiday. Lunch in those days always started with *goulash*. We loved *goulash*, too, but hardly touched it in order to remain fitter—that is to say, hungrier—for the plum-dumpling competition. About two hundred dumplings were placed in front of us, in a huge bowl; they looked like white cannon-balls—and that's what they were. We could eat an astonishing number of them, the average being around twenty. Laci, the middle one of our three cousins, was the champion with twenty-nine. My ambition was to manage twenty-five one day; like so many other ambitions in my life, this remained unfulfilled: I could never rise above an undistinguished twenty-two. Now—at this late date and thousands of miles away from Transylvania, my aunt and uncle dead and their three sons dispersed in the world—I had no hope of making up for past failures. Plum-dumplings are made of flour, potatoes, sugar and plum jam and cooked in fat—so they are among the most fattening dishes on earth. I knew that if I ate two, that would be two too many. But I watched Sam with a certain wicked anticipation.

He had very little *goulash*, which was true to tradition. The dumplings were served at last—less than two hundred, but an impressive pile, all the same. Sam proved an utter disappointment. He had one dumpling and sternly refused to touch a second one. He eyed the dumplings as Romeo eyed Juliet and Abélard eyed Heloïse; but unlike these two gentlemen, he refused to touch the object of his admiration and desire.

'Oh no, thank you,' he said firmly, almost reproaching Elza when she encouraged him to help himself. 'I don't want to kill myself, you know.'

During black coffee, the name of a lady was mentioned, and Sam remarked that she was beautiful.

'Don't be silly,' Martha told him abruptly. 'She's nearly forty.'

I looked at my watch and hoped to be able to leave soon. This was getting very unpleasant.

'Forty?' Sam retorted. 'I didn't say she was a teenager. I said she was beautiful.'

'But Martha is right,' remarked the angelic mother. 'She is much too old to be discussed as a beauty.'

She smiled a nostalgic smile and I felt that I could fall in love with her.

A few minutes later Sam left the room. Elza said she would fetch some brandy and I was left alone with Martha. She turned to me and started whispering in conspiratorial tones: 'I must talk to you. Must. *A deux*. It's vitally important.'

I was taken aback. I did not like this at all.

'Can you take me out for lunch?' she asked persistently.

'I suppose I can.'

'Tomorrow?'

'I don't see why not.'

'Tomorrow then,' she whispered. 'One o'clock at the Sea Fairy, 47th Street. And not a word to Mother or Sam.'

Elza returned to the room. We had a brandy or two, some American concoction, almost undrinkable. Sam was still out of the room. We had a third brandy and still no sign of Sam. I inquired where the bathroom was. Coming out of it, I looked into the kitchen. There was Sam, with his back to the door, sitting on a high wooden stool, devouring plum-dumplings.

He belched disgustingly and said in a blurred voice:

'Forty-three . . .'

Mariska smiled at him with pride and admiration.

He started on another dumpling.

He was breathing heavily. He belched again. He swallowed with difficulty.

'Come on, Mr MacKay,' said Mariska. 'Don't you like my plum-dumplings?'

This question was a shade too idiotic, even for Mariska.

I turned round. The two ladies of the house were standing behind me, Elza smiling benevolently, Martha looking at Sam with hatred and contempt.

'Don't I like them?' Sam repeated Mariska's question. 'Don't I? Forty-four . . .'

He stood up. He took a step towards Mariska. He tottered.

'You are the angel of the plum-dumplings . . .' he said in a frightening, deep, blurred voice.

'I'm not the Eisenhover . . .' Mariska protested.

'You're a hundred times better. You ought to be made President . . . you could win any election on a plum-dumpling ticket . . . forty-four . . . forty-four . . .'

He took a step forward and reached out for Mariska's hand, trying to kiss it. Mariska stepped back and Sam lost his balance. He fell forward with outstretched hands, saved himself by clutching at the table and swept the dish off the board—with two dumplings still left in it. The two dumplings opened up sadly, the plum jam oozing out of their insides.

It was at this point that Sam noticed the two ladies. He turned his head to examine the two dumpling casualties. Then he looked back at the two ladies again.

'Two beauties . . . Two radiant beauties . . .'

He looked at the dumplings again: 'Two other broken beauties . . .'

He laughed at his own joke.

'That's the fate of all beauties . . . they are thrown away . . . they break, and the plum jam flows out of their inside . . .'

His laughter became louder and nastier: then suddenly stopped. He nearly fell forward again but regained his balance. He sat down on the wooden chair with a heavy thump.

'Forty-four . . . forty-four . . .' he moaned.

With a deep, mournful sigh: 'Forty-f . . .'

He leaned forward and buried his face in his hands.

He had not had a drop of alcohol.

But he was roaring drunk.

3

'You must persuade Sam to marry me,' Martha Markos told me peremptorily at the Sea Fairy, even before we ordered our meal.

'I thought you hated him,' I answered, studying the menu card.

'Of course I do. But he *must* marry me.'

I looked at her in surprise. She understood and laughed aloud: 'Oh no . . not the fallen maiden. I fell to him all right . . . but no blessed event is threatening me.'

We ordered some food and I was putting ginger on a slice of melon, when she returned to the subject: 'You are wondering why I asked you to take me out for lunch.'

'I'm not. You've just told me. I must persuade Sam to marry you.'

She had a bite or two of her prawn cocktail, then pushed it aside. She looked at me: 'You really don't know anything of this story?'

'Nothing at all.'

'Then I shall tell you. But I'm surprised—it is public knowledge. I met Sam two years ago. He fell in love with me. I laughed at him for two reasons. First, because I'm a nasty character. Don't contradict me.'

'I didn't mean to.'

'You ought to have contradicted me. But don't. I could explain to you *why* I am a nasty character. I have a valid excuse, like most nasty characters. But such an explanation would not be strictly to the point. Anyway, my nasty nature was reason number one; reason number two was that I thought Sam much too old. He was thirty-nine then, I was twenty-four. He is rather a dear sometimes, quite amusing, but I found him pretty ancient as a suitor.'

'Suitor?'

'Well, first he wanted to go to bed with me—that was all. When he realised that there was nothing doing, he became so desperate that he offered marriage. I turned him down.'

'In a nasty way?'

'Yep. With sardonic laughter. Sam wouldn't take *no* for an answer and pursued me. I thought he would commit suicide.'

'You rather looked forward to it?'

'Of course I did. Who wouldn't? But Sam did nothing of the sort. Things would be so much simpler today if he had.'

'By the way, you don't want me to kill him?'

'No. That wouldn't be the same. A few months ago my mother arrived. I know she is lovely, the wretched woman; and so much nicer a person than I am. Hungarian women in New York—like all women everywhere—are trying to make themselves look younger and one of the tricks is to insist that you married awfully young. If you listen to them, you'd think Hungary was a second India: a land of child marriages. A place where girls of twelve have two or three children. But my mother *did* marry at eighteen and was only nineteen when I—her only child—was born. She is forty-five today—four years older than Sam.'

'*She* did not laugh at Sam?'

'She didn't. She started an affair with him, instead. Very discreetly, very tactfully, but right under my nose and I knew all about it. She told me, three times a week, that she was going out to play bridge. Twice she did; on the third occasion she visited Sam. On Sam-days she came home radiant and tired. No one comes home radiant *and* tired from bridge parties. It's either-or. I was half mad with jealousy. I went to inquire at the bridge salon where she was supposed to be playing and found out what I knew already, that she came only twice weekly. I even followed her once: I saw her going into the house where Sam lives. Isn't this disgusting and immoral?'

'No, it isn't.'

'I was at my wits' end. I've often heard of girls seducing their mother's lovers; but to be floored by a woman twenty years your senior? . . . And your own mother, on top of it? . . . It's unbearable.'

'You fell in love with Sam.'

'Madly. I did all I could to win him. I humiliated myself. I did my damnedest to seduce him. I succeeded. Not easily, mind you. It was jolly hard work to go to bed with the man who, not so long before, would have died for a kiss of mine. But, in the end, he condescended to sleep with me. I was passionate and behaved like an oriental concubine in a pasha's harem; he

63

was cool and perfunctory. He had betrayed my mother all right and she knew about it. She remained sweet, she always is, but suffered all the torments of hell. That gave me pleasure and cheered me up a bit. But it did not last long. Sam dropped me. He returned to Elza and would not look at me again.'

'Not even for an occasional escapade?'

'No. I'm sure he's thinking of marrying again and I'm sure he wants to marry my mother.'

'Marry *again*, you said? Isn't he a bachelor?'

'Oh, you don't know anything. He's divorced. His first wife is in Hungary. Ask him, he'll tell you all about it. Or perhaps he won't. It's quite a story but he's not fond of telling it.'

'Yours is quite a story, too. But I don't see what I can do.'

'Nor do I. Not really. But you are his friend and seem to have some influence on him. He must realise how matters stand. I love him madly.'

'Don't talk rot. You know you don't love him. You have to accept life as it comes.'

'Never!' she replied grimly.

'Bill, please,' said I to a passing waiter. Then corrected myself: 'Check!'

Before we left the table, she added thoughtfully: 'You may be right. Perhaps I don't love Sam. Perhaps I'm not mad about him. Perhaps I hate him, as we said before. Perhaps I could bear the idea of losing him.'

'Now that's a sensible girl.'

'But perhaps that's not the point. If he marries my mother, I'll kill him.'

'Don't be idotic.'

'Oh, I will. You'll see. I'll kill him all right. He has been warned.'

4

'She will have to kill me then,' Sam nodded seriously.

It was Thursday, the great day. We were travelling once again on the Long Island Railroad to Port Washington. He was nervous and keyed up. The money the State Department had paid him would last for a while, so he was not scared of the gathering clouds of financial storm, but he was very keen on his magazine idea and knew that if Borsch would not help him with it, no one else would. Borsch's unexpected pettiness and fussiness over that wretched 300 dollars a month worried him more and more as we approached our destination. He was in no mood to discuss love and marriage now; nevertheless I thought it was up to me to inform him about the lunch I had had with his girl-friend. As I was to leave next day, I could not put it off.

'She will have to kill me, then. I'm sick and tired of living alone. I know that I'll be sick and tired of married life soon enough, but *now* I'm sick and tired of loneliness. Besides, if the old misers cough up that three hundred, I'll need someone to help me with the magazine. There will be plenty to do.'

'The mother won't kill you if you marry Martha,' I suggested. 'Wouldn't that simplify matters?'

'I can't marry Martha. She's such a bitch.'

'Are you in love with Elza?'

'In love? . . . Good God! How mid-Victorian can you get? I'm talking of life, man, not of glossy magazine stories. Men at forty-one are not in love. Love is a disease, a temporary insanity, which attacks you between the ages of fifteen and twenty-five. It may return, though, throw you off balance and turn you into a ridiculous old fool at the age of sixty or so when you feel an irresistible desire to copulate with your kid secretary, or with a lecherous model or with your wife's best friend. It's just a dirty trick nature plays on you, to force you to propagate the species. Soppy novelists and cheap film producers make a good living out of this notion of love, but it should be eradicated from the vocabulary of serious, middle-aged men,

65

engaged in milking their rich friends for noble and important political purposes. You don't think I would marry a woman I was in love with?'

'Surely, other things being equal, that wouldn't prevent you from marrying her?'

'It most certainly would. Love makes you crazy and upsets your judgment. You are enchanted by silliness; you think meanness funny; you find baby-talk endearing. After three months of married life her silliness makes you scream, her meanness becomes insufferable and you feel: one more word of baby-talk and you'll strangle her. No, you make up your mind about such important matters in a cool, sober manner. I do want to get married. I think Martha is a temperamental and calculating bitch; her mother is charming, gentle, good-hearted, lovable but, alas, she loves me for my own sake.'

'No objection to that, I hope?'

'Plenty. The objection is really against myself. I could never understand those stupid middle-aged heroes of seventh-rate films who natter and whine about their souls and insist that some dull female must love them "for their own sake". Good God! My dream is that some luscious seventeen-year-old should love me for my money. But no hope of that. So what then? . . . As Elza Markos is a charming and extremely good-looking woman, only two years older than myself . . . all right, let's say three years older... as I do not want to marry her daughter; as I do want to get married; and as, finally, I have no other choice: I am going to marry Elza Markos. That is, I'm going to marry her, provided I get the required three hundred from Borsch and his flock of millionaires. Simple, isn't it? And if Martha wants to kill me—well, that's her business, not mine. Or let's say: only passively mine. I do not need to do anything about it. But don't you think we ought to give our full attention to more serious problems?'

'Welcome, gentlemen, to my humble home,' shouted P. T. Trotter, the substantial realtor, with a huge cigar in his mouth, when we entered his drawing-room. 'A dry Martini?'

Not waiting for an answer, he thrust a glass into my hand. 'My friend I.V. has talked about you. Pleased to meet you.'

'Mr Matyas is a writer,' said Borsch.

'Is he?' asked P.T. with a complete lack of interest. The only writer he knew was an advertising copywriter. A very able, very talented guy, he was told, but nothing exciting.

'You bet he is,' Borsch went on. 'His books sell in hundreds of thousands. One of his books, *The Horse Without Background*, sold two and a half million copies.'

P.T. was tremendously impressed. So was I. This was the first time I had heard about these phenomenal sales.

'Two and a half million copies!' Borsch repeated slowly, emphasising each word, pleased with the impression he had created.

'You don't say . . .' said P.T. 'That's quite something. Oh, boy. If the books cost four dollars each then—on a ten per cent basis—that is a million bucks. Gee.'

'And that's only one book,' said Borsch, trying to build me up. He was keen on showing what an illustrious man he had brought along.

'Fancy making all that dough on *books* . . .' P.T. murmured, still somewhat bemused. To make it on textiles, on ball-bearings, real estate or even on paper—which the books are printed on—that was all right; but just sitting down, writing something and making a million dollars out of it was, if not exactly immoral, at least extremely unrealistic.

'You must be a millionaire, Mr Matyas,' P.T. exclaimed admiringly.

I blushed and looked at my shoes modestly. I certainly was not one of those boastful millionaires.

Sam frowned. He had been quite pleased with my sudden rise in status: it is better to face equals; it is easier to settle these matters on a one-tycoon-to-another basis. But as soon as the word *millionaire* was uttered, he smelt danger. What if I were called upon to help his enterprise? If his magazine was to be supported by millionaires like me, it was doomed.

P.T. went on: 'I'll get my secretary, Mr Matyas, to buy a few dozen of your books. About eighty or so. Would you care to sign them?'

'Eighty books?'

'Sure. They make good Christmas presents, particularly when signed by the author. Who sells two and a half million. Gee.'

'Yes, I'll sign them with pleasure, Mr Trotter.'

'Just call me P.T. I don't care for formalities. D'you mind if I call you Peter?'

As my name is Michael, I did mind a bit, but I did not say so.

'Delighted.'

'I'll get all your books, Peter, and I'll put a set of them in my library.'

I smiled even more modestly than before.

'That's what I'll do. Not only will I buy your books, but I'll most certainly put them in my library.'

I thought of asking where he kept his other books—those which he did not want to honour specially. But I said nothing.

Sam was engaged in a conversation with Earl F. Millington, an oil man.

'You are Hungarian, Mr MacKay, I'm told,' said Earl F. Millington.

Sam admitted it in manly fashion.

'Plenty of Hungarians down my parts, in Cleveland, Ohio. We call them Magyars sometimes. Don't know who invented this name for them but that's what we call them sometimes down there.'

'No offence meant, I'm sure,' said Sam understandingly.

'Sure not,' exclaimed Earl F. Millington. 'We just give these funny names to people. But we like our Magyars down there,

68

in Cleveland, Ohio. We call the Germans *krauts* and the Italians *kikes*. But we respect them immensely.'

'Sure we do,' agreed P.T., a little doubtfully.

'We have all sorts of people in Cleveland, Ohio,' Earl F. Millington explained. 'All nationalities. You see, Mr MacKay, this blessed land of ours is quite a . . . quite a . . .' He searched for a word, then at last, he found it: 'Quite a melting pot!'

'If you may coin a phrase,' Sam nodded. Earl F. Millington was pleased by Sam's appreciative remark.

'We have Hungarians, Germans, Italians . . .'

He stopped, having run out of nationalities. He tried again:

'And Czecho-Slavs . . . and . . . and . . . Yugo-Slovaks—'

'And Ukrainians . . . Scandinavians . . . White Russians . . . White Tyrolians . . .' Sam helped him out politely.

'Sure, Mr MacKay,' Earl F. Millington shouted gratefully. 'The whole damn lot. How did you know? Been to Cleveland, Ohio?'

'Not yet. But I've read about it.'

'Sure you have. It's quite a melting pot, believe me, sir.'

'Gee,' remarked P.T.

As I too felt the need to contribute to the conversation, I said: 'Gee!'

More dry Martinis were poured out to all, except to Mrs Leo Doros, who did not drink. The conversation rambled on pointlessly. The three other tycoons also made their contributions—and proved that they were the spiritual equals of Earl F. Millington. Sam grew more and more impatient. At last, Wilberforce S. Schmalz, P.T.'s lawyer, broached the subject.

'We are pleased to learn, Mr MacKay, that you wish to intensify the Cold War and give the Reds hell.'

This was the last thing Sam wanted to do but he knew better than to argue and to try to explain ideas in this company.

'You bet,' he said instead.

'To give hell to all Reds and dangerous liberals,' said Borsch, partly to reassure his friends, partly to underline the fact that he did belong.

Earl F. Millington, who was apparently fond of enumerating things, was off again: 'Communists, Trotsky-ites, socialists, liberals, pacifists, Buddhists, neurotics . . . The whole damn lot.'

'You bet,' Sam repeated, feeling that he had found the right phrase.

'Since poor Joe McCarthy is fading,' said Wilberforce S. Schmalz, the attorney, 'we feel that we must do something to strengthen the front of Upright Christianity and keep the flag flying.'

'Good man, Senator McCarthy,' one of the other millionaires, a ladies' underwear manufacturer, remarked.

'A great and good guy,' Earl F. Millington agreed.

'He made mistakes,' said the attorney, thus showing a remarkable independence of mind.

'He shouldn't have attacked the army,' said Borsch.

'The best army in the world,' nodded the underwear manufacturer.

'Sure it is the best army,' Earl F. Millington shouted. 'Nothing comes near it in the whole world. But all damned generals are dangerous Reds.'

'That's true,' P.T. agreed. 'That they sure are.'

'The gentlemen present here,' the attorney continued, 'and another half dozen of their generous and far-seeing friends, recognise the Red menace, threatening our Christian civilisation, and are determined to take up the cudgel.'

'You bet,' said one of the minor millionaires.

The attorney proceeded: 'Your plan seems to be most acceptable and it forms a sound basis for our activities. We want the magazine; we fully approve [slight bow to the shrunken little lady] of the idea of the Leo Doros Prize; and we have two or three little ideas of our own. We are going to form a little

Trust Foundation and I shall have the honour of looking after the legal side.'

'They are mad,' Sam whispered to me in Hungarian.

'They are going to give you the money, it seems,' I replied. 'Never mind the legal side.'

'Please come to my office, Mr MacKay, at eleven o'clock tomorrow morning and we shall settle some formalities. Among other matters, we shall have to pay in this cheque for three hundred to the Foundation's new account. It's drawn on the Foundation you see. But, in order to express these gentlemen's appreciation of your ideas and as a sign of their goodwill and trust, I now hand this cheque for three hundred over to you. Don't forget to bring it along tomorrow morning.'

He stepped forward.

'Very good luck to you, and to the Trust for Christian Civilisation.'

He handed the cheque to Sam with a wide and pompous gesture. Sam was embarrassed. He felt he ought to make a speech but he also felt the situation too silly for words.

'Gentlemen . . .' he began.

Then, with a graceful bow towards Mrs Leo Doros, he corrected himself: 'My lady, and gentlemen . . . With your generous gift here . . .'

He lifted the cheque and looked at it casually, for the first time. His eyes popped out. His hands began to tremble.

'Ouaaah . . .' he moaned. His knees gave way and he collapsed. He lay there on the carpet, stretched out at full length as if dead, still clinging to the cheque.

Borsch jumped up, poured a glass of water from a crystal jug, lifted Sam's head and tried to make him sip a little.

'Give me a piece of ice . . .' he asked Earl F. Millington.

I knelt down to have a look at the cheque.

I nearly fainted, too.

It was for 300,000 dollars.

Apparently, when we talked of 'three hundred' it never even

entered anybody's mind that we were not counting in megabucks. Later I felt sure that if they had ever suspected that we wanted only three hundred dollars, they would have kicked us out without a cent.

Next day I left for London, leaving Sam to cope with his new problems and worries.

THE APPRENTICE'S BROOM

I

I was busy in London after my return from America, having been commissioned to turn *King Lear* into a musical. I started work with a composer called Egbert Troth. Right at the beginning we had a big row with our producer who thought that our number, when Lear's three daughters on their first entrance came in dancing and singing, 'Three little girls of Lear are we', was strongly reminiscent of *The Mikado*. I was also busy adapting Hagias's *Homeward Voyage*—a most amusing Greek comedy of the second century B.C.—into iambic verse, for the Third Programme. A similar adaptation of mine, the *Cyprian Lays*, based, it is needless to remind the reader, on Stasinus's original, had been a roaring success shortly before. Audience research showed that we had more than forty listeners, an unprecedented number for this type of programme. I was also discussing the outlines of a science fiction novel with one of the less highbrow paper-back firms. In my synopsis three men —Hungarian refugees—had managed to land on the moon. They were in the belief that they were the first human beings to reach the place but in fact, another bunch of Hungarian refugees was already there, waiting for them. That's where complications started. The director of the paper-back firm thought the story improbable; he knew little about Hungarian refugees.

On top of it all, I had a visit from a Persian publisher who wanted to bring out a school edition of my best-seller, *Horse Without Background* in English with annotations in Persian. The Iranian publisher and I signed the contract and afterwards went out (on expense account) to discuss its details over dinner at the Savoy Grill; from there we went on to a striptease joint, still on expense account, to clarify further details of the contract which was already on its way to Persia. It was three o'clock in the morning when I got home.

I had hardly dropped off to sleep, when the telephone rang, and the operator announced a personal call for me. On pressing inquiries he managed to find out that it was from the Trust of Christian Civilisation, New York. The caller proved to be Sam. I had not heard from him for weeks and weeks. He sounded cheerful, but very matter of fact.

'I say,' said he, 'do you want to go to Bermuda?'

'What? . . . Where to? . . .'

'Bermuda.'

'What for?'

'Oh, it's a conference of some sort.'

'On what?'

'Oh, something or other, it doesn't matter what. I think it's about the Church. Or cruelty to fish. I'm not quite sure. You would go, of course, at the T.C.C.'s expense.'

'You're joking!'

'Good heavens, no. I'm dead serious.'

I was still terribly sleepy but anger started waking me up.

'Listen, Sam, I'm a fairly easy-going chap. But to ring me up at three o'clock in the morning . . .'

'Jeez,' he exclaimed; he sounded genuinely concerned. 'I quite forgot about the time lag. How stupid of me! It's only ten o'clock here. Sorry, old man. It's unforgivable. I should have known better. I'll ring tomorrow. Sleep well.'

He put the receiver down. The 'sleep well' sounded ironical. He did not ring next morning, nor at any time the next day. Nor ever again. Four weeks later, I received a telegram from him:

ARRIVING WEDNESDAY 2 P.M. LONDON AIRPORT WITH MY WIFE STOP PARTLY BUSINESS PARTLY HONEYMOON STOP PLEASE RESERVE ROOM IN ONE OF TOP HOTELS SAM

This telegram, of course, puzzled me greatly. He had never

74

told me about his marriage to Elza. I was pleased to find that in spite of Martha's threats he was still alive. Or had he married Martha, after all? I dismissed the thought. He always talked most disparagingly of her. He was not afraid of Elza being four years his senior. But why this abrupt way of breaking the news? Why had he sent me no announcement?

On Wednesday I drove out to the dilapidated prefabricated huts which constituted the long-distance terminal at London Airport. Sam's plane was dead on time, which meant it was only seventeen minutes late. It was a pleasant summer day and I walked out to the terrace adjoining the restaurant, to watch the plane land. It taxied along the tarmac and stopped right below me. Sam must have spotted me from the plane. He gave no sign of recognition but he arranged his entry with high histrionic skill. He was about the tenth passenger to appear at the top of the gantry stairs. I thought he was a little plumper than last time. He descended two or three steps, then turned back and shouted gaily:

'Hurry up, Eisenhower!'

He was followed by a red-faced and pleasantly beaming Mariska.

2

'Do you know Goethe?' Sam asked me.

'Which one?'

'What do you mean which one?'

'Do you mean Johann Wolfgang Goethe, the celebrated late German poet or Melvin P. Goethe, the American writer of dirty songs?'

'I mean Johann Wolfgang,' said Sam dryly.

'I know Melvin P. better,' I told him. 'But I know Johann W., too.'

We were in his office, a fortnight after their arrival. They had a suite in the Dorchester and his sitting-room was being used as a temporary office. He had not shown himself any too eager to see me; in fact, we had not met since I drove him in from the airport. I thought he might want to disclose some further details of the Bermuda trip; or offer some explanation about his somewhat unexpected marriage, but he did not feel the necessity. I rang him once or twice after his arrival but he was always busy, so I desisted. Then one day he telephoned me and asked if I could come along to his hotel.

'You know that famous and over-quoted poem, the *Zauberlehrling*, the *Sorcerer's Apprentice*,' said Sam. 'The young apprentice, copying his master, orders a broom to take a bucket and fetch water from the well. It works. The broom obeys his command and goes back and forth for more and more water. And the apprentice does not know how to stop it. It goes on fetching water, until the house is flooded.'

'The story,' I nodded, 'is not entirely new to me.'

'I'm the Sorcerer's Apprentice,' he declared grimly. 'I'm flooded with money. I am at my wits' end.'

I stared at him.

'The money we raised in Port Washington—the cheque you saw—was only the beginning. The broom's very first visit to the well. Now it keeps going back for fresh supplies and I don't know the spell to stop it. I don't even dare to try; I'm supposed to look overjoyed. Borsch and his pals—Wilberforce S. Schmalz, the attorney, is really the chief villain of the piece—have gone on with the collection. And as more and more underwear manufacturers, share-pushers, real estate speculators and some genuine big industrialists are hell bent on proving how determined they are to save Western civilisation, the fund has risen slowly to over half a million dollars. And it's still rising. If we get much more money, I'll be ruined.'

'Surely, it's not all *your* responsibility.'

'Oh no . . . They have a most impressive Committee of great men as well as crooks and phoneys. Jocelyn Herb, the short-story writer, the G.O.M. of American literature is the Chairman of the Committee. He is ninety-seven and the vigour of his mind and his perceptive powers are not what they used to be sixty or seventy years ago. Mrs Leo Doros is one of the Vice-Presidents. A Professor of Philosophy from one of the Ivy League Universities is another Vice-President. A former assistant secretary of the Treasury—one of the most intelligent and honest men in the United States but a friend of P. T. Trotter —is listed next to an eminently successful income-tax evader. Borsch's name comes after that of a retired Supreme Court Judge. A mixed lot, you might say. They can get the best names from Europe, too. Nobel Prize winners and Archbishops are awaiting an invitation with bated breath. They are convinced, poor lambs, that the money is being used for some decent and worthy cause. And that's where the complication sets in: the money, after all, *may* be used for a decent and worthy cause. Our rules don't forbid it.'

'Well, then go and find worthy causes,' said I. 'What's the problem?'

'Plenty of problems. First, as long as they look on me as a sort of Chief of General Staff in this set-up, I can't really do what I like. But the main problem simply is: how to spend all that money.'

'Give me a thousand. Or if you think I am mean and not helpful enough, give me two thousand. Give me three.'

Sam shook his head in disapproval.

'It's no good being facetious. You know how it is with large organisations. It does not matter how much you spend as long as it looks all right on the books. I may spend £3,000 on an utterly senseless journey to Patagonia; but if I claim so much as 15 cents on liquorice gums, there is a major rumpus and top-level investigation and I'll lose my job. I can spend £2,000 on entertainment . . .'

'Give me £2,000. It would entertain me no end.'

Sam looked at me grimly.

'Don't treat this as a joke.'

'But why not, for God's sake?' I began to lose my temper.

'This is not very serious. It's rather fun, in fact. The whole thing started as a timid effort to scrape a few pennies together for a refugee magazine and it ends with hundreds of thousands of dollars in hand. . . ."

Sam groaned painfully.

'Don't rub it in . . .' he said, but I paid no notice to him.

'I can't shed bitter tears over that. If it's too much for you, chuck it. Just get out and forget all about it.'

'You don't understand,' Sam replied with a certain gravity. 'I can't chuck it because it has certain potentialities. I may be able to do something good, although I doubt it. It's my job, too, and I haven't got another. But the main point is this: once a vast organisation like that comes into existence, it starts living its own life. It's like a book: if a book comes to life at all, it lives a life quite independent of its author. It's a work; it's there; it's public property. It interprets itself or anybody can interpret it freely—anybody, that is, except the author, who has had his say. Similarly, the T.C.C. is an entity now. It has been brought to life and has a right to live. It has to be fed. It wants to do *something*—no matter what. I've become a cog in the machine. The apprentice's broom, all over again. The money *must* be spent.'

'And what if you don't spend it? If some money is left over for next year?'

'But that's quite out of the question. That goes against the grain. Then they cut down our allocation. They'd say: half a million is too much? Very well, we'll give you 300,000 next year. And they do—and then there we are.'

'Where? Isn't 300,000 too much as it is?'

'No. Not if you put it that way. But if you can get half a million, you need 600,000; if you get 600,000 you can't manage under a million. That's part of the eternal law. The apprentice's broom again. All the money they give you *must* be spent. And at least fifteen per cent more.'

I suddenly remembered how back in New York Sam had

been cowed by Lucky Strike advertisements into giving up Chesterfields. I reminded him of this.

'Yes, you're right, I am a weak character. Perhaps I always do what people *expect* me to do. Or even what an institution expects me to do. The tyrant here isn't Borsch, or P.T., or Schmalz; the tyrant is the organisation, determined to live its own life, determined to enslave me and trample me down.'

'Has the little Hungarian magazine started yet?' I asked.

'God, no. It's off. Who has time for little Hungarian magazines? I am busy founding magazines here in London, in Paris, in Italy, in Holland and Sweden. Maybe one in Ukrainian and one in Schwitzerdutsch too. Up to now, Schwitzerdutsch has been only a spoken language; we're going to turn it into a written one. Who can say, after that, that we have not done something for Christian Civilisation?'

3

'Oh, it's all right—Mr Matyas's party. You don't need a number,' said the cloakroom attendant when she took our coats in the Paprika.

'Thank you, Mabel,' said I, a little condescendingly perhaps, to underline my familiarity with the place.

It was the first time I'd been out to have a meal with the MacKays, a few weeks after my chat with Sam. He had still offered me no explanation of his matrimonial adventure. But he told me all about it later that night while Mariska was crying in the lavatory.

The evening started pleasantly enough.

'How do you like London?' I asked her.

'I like it,' she replied pleasantly as always. 'I liked New York, I liked Kis-Harsany, why shouldn't I like London? What's the difference?'

Sam chuckled. 'There *is* a difference, Mariska, if you come to think of it more deeply,' he said gently.

'There's one thing wrong here,' she admitted. 'I've got nothing to do.'

'You see, Mariska likes running a house,' Sam explained, 'and here we're living in a hotel. That upsets her a bit.'

'I haven't even made scrambled eggs for weeks,' she grumbled.

The trouble began during the main course. The proprietor of the Paprika—a burly, middle-aged man who never stopped rubbing his hands—walked round the restaurant, bowing to his clients, pausing to talk with those he knew personally. He had started as a waiter but now he was rich, proud of the Paprika's good reputation and much more interested in well-informed praise than in making another pound or two. We told him that the food was as good as ever and waited for him to go on to the next table. He noticed, however, that Sam was just starting on a steak à la Bakony.

'I'm just trying a new kind of paprika sauce with that. I wonder what you think of it, Mr MacKay?'

'Very good,' said Sam.

This sounded a little off-hand and the proprietor wanted more reassurance.

'You don't really like it, Mr MacKay. You are only being polite.'

Sam, keen to go on chatting with me, was anxious to get rid of the proprietor. But the latter, noticing that Sam was eating much less than usual, grew concerned.

'You don't think there is too much sour cream in it?' he asked anxiously.

Sam was getting fed up.

'There isn't,' he replied with exaggerated warmth. 'I assure you, this is the best paprika sauce I ever tasted.'

Sam and the proprietor went on being technical about the ingredients and consistency of the sauce, when I noticed that Mariska was sobbing.

I asked her: 'Anything wrong, Mariska?'

She did not reply. Suddenly she jumped up from the table and ran out of the restaurant. The proprietor followed her in panic.

Sam stood up after a pause and was about to follow her. At the door he met the proprietor coming back.

'Mrs MacKay has gone into the powder-room.'

Sam returned to our table.

'A damn stupid thing to say,' he grumbled. 'The best sauce I ever tasted my foot. Compared with Mariska's sauce it's dish-water.'

He lit a cigarette.

'She's jealous,' he said. 'She loves me.'

After some reflection, he added: 'Other women are jealous of saucy *reds*; she is jealous of a red sauce.'

This, I felt, was not the time for puns. I waved to a waiter but when he approached our table, Sam got in first: 'Will you please find out if my wife is still in the ladies' room and if so, what she is doing there.'

The waiter gave us a bewildered look. He came back presently: 'The lady has locked herself in one of the . . . in one of the cubicles and is sobbing loudly.'

'Go in after her,' I suggested.

'In the ladies' lavatory, sir?'

I had to admit that he had a point there.

'Too early, in any case,' Sam added. 'Let her sob a bit.'

We smoked in silence. After a while, I asked him; 'Why did you marry her?'

After a long pause, he answered: 'Because I'm basically an honest man.'

This sounded cryptic but I asked no further questions. He went on, without being asked: 'There were too many scenes with Martha. She became unbearable. No doubt you remember our evening at their place. Next time I went to see them, Martha accused me of getting drunk on plum-dumplings. Perhaps she was right. On another occasion, in a fit of fury, she told me that I was frequenting their house on false pretences. "Not because you're having an affair with my aged mother, which would be bad enough; but even that would be more honest . . . You don't come here for mother's sake. You come only for Mariska." That set me thinking. A few days afterwards, I was in bed with the old lady. She was worried because of her daughter's undisguised hostility. There, lying in bed, she looked into my eyes and asked in her quiet gentle way: "Tell me one thing, Sam: why don't you marry Mariska?" I thought this over. I decided the two women were right. I was persuaded. "I shall," I replied. And I did.'

'Just like that?'

'Just like how can you marry people? You know the old joke about the man complaining about his wife? "I wanted to marry a woman," he says, "who is a lady in the drawing-room, a cook in the kitchen and a cocotte in the bedroom. Alas, I've got someone who is a cocotte in the drawing-room, a lady in the kitchen and a cook in the bedroom." This is a frightening little tale, with a moral. I was determined to avoid this mistake. So I did the honest thing—that's what I was referring to. I really want a cook; I need a cook; I married a cook. She is a cook everywhere: in the drawing-room as well as in the bedroom but—thank God—she *is* a cook in the kitchen, too. Many people marry cooks but they are utterly dishonest about it. Trying to cheat the world and themselves. Not me.'

'Love doesn't come into it at all? Well, you did explain that to me once. You've never been in love in your life? With women, I mean. Not with shoulders of lamb.'

He smiled a melancholy smile.

'Yes, I have. Once. With a woman. I married that woman, too. I was madly in love with her. But she cured me of the disease of love all right, thank you very much. Never again. But I'd rather not talk about it, if you don't mind. . . But I *shall* remain faithful to shoulders of lamb; and if I want a change, if I feel like being unfaithful, I turn to legs of chicken and goose-liver. I am a happy man,' he added. 'I wish she did not sometimes call me Mr MacKay, even nowadays; but, sooner or later, she will get out of that habit. Yes, on the whole, I'm a happy man.'

'How did Martha take it?' I asked.

'Badly. She made frightful scenes about my pinching her cook—in every sense of the word. She had never thought of this possibility, she said, although it was she who first put the idea in my head. She told me she'd have preferred it if I had taken her mother instead.'

'I don't believe she would,' I replied. 'She'll calm down. She'll get over the loss of Mariska.'

'Never. She said she would fight to get her back. And if things go on like this, one day she may.'

'Why? Apart from this little incident—they don't go well?'

'How could they? I married a cook and turned her into a lady of leisure. She has nothing to do; she has nowhere to cook. And as far as I am concerned, I hardly dare to eat because she is so jealous of other people's cooking. You saw me here tonight. I had a soup; that unfortunate steak à la Bakony; and these two pancakes. Is *that* a supper for me? It's like Fangio driving at twenty miles an hour. Like Bannister running an eight-minute mile. I just don't know what to do.'

'You are sillier than I thought, Sam,' I told him. 'It's the simplest thing on earth: give her a chance to cook again. That's what she wants; that's what you want; it will make both of you happy again.'

He watched the smoke of his cigarette for a long time.

'Perhaps,' he agreed.

He asked Mabel, the cloakroom attendant, to pay a visit to his wife, give her his kind regards and ask her to come out.

'Your wife says,' Mabel reported, returning from her errand, 'that she will never come out.'

'Never?' asked Sam doubtfully.

'Never. That's what she said. She sounded quite determined.'

'Have you heard anything like that before?' exclaimed Sam.

'One lady said something like that three years ago. But she came out all right after three days.'

Sam asked Mabel to return to Mariska: 'Please tell her that it was all a misunderstanding. Her paprika sauce is easily the best in the world. Tell her—listen carefully, Mabel—tell her that even Eisenhower couldn't make a better sauce than she can. Never mind what this means; just tell her. And tell her that tomorrow we are going to leave the hotel and move into a furnished apartment. With a kitchen of her own.'

Three minutes later a still tearful but beaming Mariska appeared: 'I'll cook paprika chicken for you tomorrow. Just to show you what a real sauce tastes like.' She lowered her voice seductively: 'And you can have plum-dumplings afterwards.'

4

I had to work hard on *King Lear* (it had been decided that the musical version would be called *Oh My Papa*) and did not see much of Sam. He moved into a furnished flat in South Audley Street and looked not only happy and content but also a quarter of an inch wider in circumference, every time we met.

He travelled a great deal. He kept hopping over to the Continent and eventually the various magazines started appearing: *Die Brücke* in Germany, *Le Pont* in France, *Il Ponte* in Italy, *Bron* in Sweden, *De Brug* in Holland and *Brückli*, the Schwitzerdutsch version. *A Hid*, the little Hungarian magazine originally planned, had long been forgotten. Once he flew back to New York, too, in order, I think, to stem the flood of money, but he was not too successful in that. But *The Bridge*, the English magazine, was a great success from Sam's point of view and he was delighted with it. It was losing almost as much money single-handed as the other five put together.

He was very lucky in his choice of editor. Crispian Ransome-Hall was a serious and devoted man, a B.A. of Leicester

University and cut out for the job. His face was pink and he spat in all directions when talking excitedly—which he always did. He felt passionately on every subject under the sun and his conscience was always troubled. He was very proud of his working-class origins and spoke a great deal—spitting all the time—about his early years of hunger and deprivation in County Durham. His father was a miner and he was fond of relating how during the years of unemployment the old man spent three years in Strangeways Prison for causing grievous bodily harm to a mining official. The old man's name was simply John Hall, he explained, and his real name was also John Hall. He had picked Crispian plus the double-barrelled version of his surname in an ill-advised outburst of snobbery which he now regretted.

One of his enemies—and he had many—dug out an early piece of writing by Ransome-Hall which had appeared in a Northern newspaper before the nation-wide snobbery about low-class origins really got into its stride, in which he described his father as an honest grocer in Durham. This was a heavy blow to Ransome-Hall's prestige, but not long afterwards he would have been only too pleased to compromise on a father in the grocery business. An old friend of the family—a music critic who knew his father well and whose contributions had been rejected by *The Bridge*—spread the terrible libellous news that Crispian's father was really a solicitor in Manchester. His son's real name *was* Crispian Ransome-Hall and the old boy was a pillar of middle-class respectability and a backbone of old England. Nor had he ever seen the inside of Strangeways Prison, not even to visit a client. Young Crispian once went to stay with a spinster aunt in Durham but she disliked the boy's habit of spitting and never asked him again. That one brief visit was Crispian's entire connection with County Durham. His Northern accent was a fake, too. His normal accent was the usual, innocuous speech of Leicester, where he went to university. When he got worked up, he forgot his laboriously acquired Northern accent and spoke like a B.B.C. announcer.

The fact remained that spitting and a Northern accent were mutually exclusive. Crispian, when excited, started spitting and spoke B.B.C.; when calm—however rare an occurrence—he refrained from spraying his interlocutors and talked as he imagined people in a Muggleswick pub did.

But Crispian's origins were of no interest to Sam. As far as Sam was concerned, he was a godsend; he was about the most incompetent and spendthrift editor in the world. He was very vain and, being a frustrated poet, was keen on being praised and admired by everyone. He took people out for lunch six times a week and commissioned articles on every subject under the sun from all and sundry. On one occasion he lunched with seven Cambridge undergraduates and ordered essays from all seven, thus managing to get rid of about £350 plus the expenses of a sumptuous meal for eight, in one hour. He had enough material on his desk to fill the magazine for three years without purchasing anything else—and that after only a few months of existence. This mania for buying and pleasing people was coupled with another virtue: he was untidy and inefficient and lost or mislaid a considerable proportion of the manuscripts entrusted to his care. He sent them to readers, illustrators, translators, friends, and never got them back; and he could never remember, when attacked by angry authors, where these pieces had got to. His clients raged; as he never answered letters and never called people back on the telephone, they raged even more. To pacify them, he took them out to lunch and commissioned them to write another piece or two.

'He's worth his weight in gold,' Sam was in the habit of saying.

But Crispian's virtues did not end even there. He produced an extremely highbrow and unbearably dull magazine. All the obscure professors in all the obscure universities and all the highbrow writers with tiny but devoted followings—two or three people as a rule—made a point of appearing in *The Bridge*. The magazine had a great reputation and a circulation of 1,200 copies. Of these, four hundred were actually paid for, and of the four hundred, almost one hundred were even read or at least scanned. The estimated readership was actually four hundred persons, and to keep his Four Hundred well apprised of world affairs, Crispian travelled all over the globe. He visited every trouble spot, interviewed countless statesmen, members of parliament, British High Commissioners, foreign ambassadors, spitting in their eyes and explaining *their* particular problems to them with terrifying verbosity— and then printing what he himself had said as *their* views. When Adenauer was invited to Russia (in June, 1955) he travelled to Moscow before him, and analysed the situation for the benefit of the Four Hundred; when a naval revolt was defeated in Argentina, he flew to Buenos Aires; when the coalition government resigned in Italy, he travelled to Rome. He was present at Strasbourg at the first meeting of the Assembly of Western European Union. It was a sore point that he failed to turn up in Belgrade during the Canossa visit of Messrs Bulganin and Khrushchev. The sole reason for this was his physical inability to be at two places at one and the same time. However, he managed to visit Budapest and report on the thaw and the struggle between Rakosi and Imre Nagy. Soon afterwards he flew to Ghana, or the Gold Coast as it then was, to collect secret first-hand information on the activities of the National Liberation Movement. Between such visits he hurried home, to buy more useless manuscripts.

Sam thought the world of him but Crispian Ransome-Hall was not a happy man. As a writer he was reasonably successful but he knew, as so many do, at the bottom of his heart, that he was a sham. He was the author of the definitive biography of John Pomfret (1667-1703), a long essay on Reginald Pecock (1395-1460) and he had once been lecturer in English at a colonial university (1952-54). He was also the favourite novelreviewer of the *Sunday Post* because he could squeeze reviews on ninety-eight books into forty lines while his nearest rival could not deal with more than fifty. As I have said, he regarded himself, in spite of all these accomplishments, as a failure. He wanted to shine as a poet and as a poet he was a washout. He could find no publisher for his volume, *Lightbrown Thursdays*, and he was only too painfully aware that poetic public opinion held him in derision. The young poets grouped around the *Hillock* magazine jeered at him; the *Gaze* people once called him a Georgian, the gravest of all insults in those circles. In fact, the young poets he held in esteem were so contemptuous of him that they refused to submit poems to *The Bridge*. They needed money badly but they refused to accept *his* money. Their integrity humiliated him even more.

On one occasion, one of Crispian's poems—'Tophats and Canaries'—was published in *Peace and People*, the organ of a Communist front organisation. The sole reason for this was that 'Tophats and Canaries' was rejected by all other organs but was accepted by *Peace and People*. From that moment onwards, however, young poets declared that Ransome-Hall was a dangerous fellow-traveller; others—or indeed, often the same people in different surroundings—maintained that he was a hireling and instrument of American dollar-imperialism.

One day Sam dropped in to me because he had had some shattering news. His American patrons—Borsch, P. T. Trotter and the others—had managed to rope in some more big industrialists and still larger sums of money were now reaching T.C.C.'s New York account.

'What will you do?' I asked him, full of sympathy.

'As an immediate counter-measure, I'm sending Ransome-Hall to Israel to report on the post-election situation. From there he'll go to Brazil, to cover the presidential elections. Then he will come home and buy more useless manuscripts, with renewed vigour and devotion. Good man, Ransome-Hall. Of course this will not solve my problem. But I have an answer ready to those fiends in New York, don't you worry. I'm going to organise a congress in Sorrento and invite two hundred and fifty eminent literary and academic figures of our age.'

'What will be the theme of the congress?'

'The relationship between Eastern and Western Culture.'

'Why?'

'For one reason only,' he replied with a wicked grin. 'With a subject like that I can invite lots of eggheads from Japan, Hong Kong and such places. And a return ticket from Tokyo costs more than £400.'

He beamed with satisfaction.

But he knew nothing of Sir Henry Salami as yet.

5

When I lifted the receiver an authoritative female voice ordered me to hold on. After a long pause, she asked me: 'Are you there?' I said I was. After another minute or two she came back and asked me what I wanted. I told her that she had rung me. 'Oh . . .' she said in a voice which implied: 'Some people are hopelessly stupid,' and then, after a further interval, she declared: 'I'll connect you now.'

I knew these telephone calls, I get a dozen a day like this. They come from publishers, or other businessmen. After such preliminaries one knows that one is connected to the great man's secretary or to his secretary's secretary. Today I was in luck: I was connected straight to the secretary herself.

'This is Mr Enrico Salami's secretary,' she cooed. 'Mr Salami wishes to know if you could dine at his house at 7.15 on Wednesday?'

I should have said no, of course. If he wants me, let him ring me up himself. But I knew that the dinner would be excellent and I am also interested in revisiting rich men's homes.

'I'd like to, but Wednesday is a bit difficult for me. I'd prefer some other day,' said I, trying to be awkward.

'It must be Wednesday,' she said coolly.

'All right, Wednesday then,' I gave in meekly. But to save the last crumb of my self-respect, I added: 'On Wednesday I can't make it before 7.45, though.'

'That's rather late for Mr Salami,' said the school-mistressy voice at the other end.

'I can't manage earlier,' I replied stubbornly.

'Very well. At 7.45 then, on Wednesday.'

I had no idea what Enrico Salami wanted from me. He was a very rich man. He had something to do with sausages and that rather endeared him to me because I love sausages. He was the prototype of the self-made business tycoon, for which I also liked him. Forty years before, he had come from Italy as a penniless immigrant. When I had met him at a wedding reception years before, he had told me he had enjoyed reading *Horse Without Background*. Could we meet again? His secretary rang me soon afterwards and made a dinner appointment. Then I met Mrs Salami too, and several more very rich and very dull men with their even duller wives, liberally adorned with jewellery. They talked of real estate prices, take-over bids, super-tax and square feet. I found Enrico Salami a little primitive too, but he was amiable and sincere and a lot better than the rest. We parted bosom friends, he said repeatedly that we must meet again soon. I agreed that we must. Absolutely. But I had heard nothing from him again until now.

When I arrived at 7.45, the Italian butler took my hat and coat and led me into a large and beautiful library furnished with exquisite taste. Enrico's private secretary received me, offered me a drink, asked me to sit down and left me alone. I admired Enrico's pictures; he collected seventeenth-century Italians— a rare choice but more refreshing perhaps than the ubiquitous Impressionists which all millionaires have come to regard as obligatory.

A minute later Enrico burst into the room, greeted me effusively, asked me what I had been up to since he had seen me last, offered me another drink, poured out a tomato juice for himself and then asked me: 'You know that man Sam MacKay?'

'Good friend of mine.'

'That's what I thought. Can you introduce him to me?'

'I could . . .' I told him, reluctantly.

'You know something of this Trust for Christian Civilisation, too? T.C.C.?'

'I know everything about the T.C.C. And a little more.'

'A little more than everything? . . . Hahaha . . . That's good. You *are* a great wit. Well, you must bring this Sam MacKay along. I want to give him money.'

That was what I had feared.

'You can't do that, Enrico,' I said. 'Please.'

'What d'you mean "You can't do that, Enrico"? Why? Doesn't he need money?'

'No. He has too much of it as it is. Can't you give it to some other organisation? Plenty of deserving causes.'

He shook his head firmly.

'Dogs? Cats?' I suggested.

'No.'

'Birds?'

'No.'

'Fishes?'

'It must be the T.C.C. I want to go into this charity racket properly and in a big way. Good causes are few and far between. And most of them are in hand. Dogs? Surely, you know I can't butt in on old Lord Shamrock. Cats? I won't play second fiddle to Mrs Leonard. I'm telling you, I went through the lot. All good causes are firmly in hand and people won't let them go. The T.C.C. is new in this country. Virgin soil. If I dilly-dally, someone else will snatch it. It is a little political, and it also has a literary touch: just what I want. MacKay will have to take my money whether he likes it or not. Sorry.'

He sounded quite fierce.

'How much do you have in mind?' I asked, suspecting the worst.

'A hundred thousand. That is, a hundred thousand at first. Then I'll see.'

'Hm . . .' I shook my head. 'You couldn't make it fifty, I suppose?'

91

'I'll start with a hundred,' he repeated it cruelly.

'Dollars?'

'Pounds.'

I shrugged my shoulders. 'MacKay won't like it.'

'That's his funeral,' Enrico declared callously.

Mrs Salami joined us for dinner but after a wonderful meal we retired, just the two of us again, to the library and over coffee and brandy—he had coffee and tomato juice—he explained: 'I'll tell you quite frankly. I don't want you to repeat this to anyone but I want you to know. I have two good reasons for this. First of all, I want some respect. Real respect. I want people to stop laughing at me.'

'Who is laughing at you?'

'Everybody. Percy Markham, the brewer, for example. Just because I deal in intestines. Is that so funny?'

'You deal in what?' I asked him, greatly surprised.

'Intestines. Didn't you know?'

'I always thought you dealt in sausages. Why should anyone buy intestines?'

'Don't be so damned ignorant. Have you never stopped to think how sausages are made? The sausage meat has to be filled into something. That something is intestines. Pigs' or lambs', as a rule. It's big business. I grew rich on intestines. Nowadays we use mostly artificial materials but intestines are still bought and sold. All my friends make endless jokes about this. Markham always starts sniffing about when he sees me. As though I smelt. I assure you, his beer stinks more than my intestines.'

He was quite worked up.

'I thought big money never stank,' I told him. 'Or it always does. The point is, I thought people laughed at a rag-and-bone man, but never at a scrap-iron millionaire. As soon as a person has the first million he ceases to be funny and becomes respectable. That's what I always thought.'

'They still laugh at me. And they also laugh at me because of my name. It's an honourable name. And an ancient one. I come from a long line of Salamis. I think it is stupid and childish to laugh at a name in any case. But I shall stop them laughing. I'll go into this charity racket, because I want a knighthood. And that's my second ambition.'

Sir Henry Salami, flashed through my mind. I liked the sound and the rhythm of the name. For me, he became Sir Henry Salami then and there.

'I know it's childish,' he went on. 'Maybe it is. But I want a title. I must have a title. That will stop Mr Markham laughing.'

His eyes flashed with anger. He stood up and poured out another tomato juice for himself. He also lit a cigar.

'I came to this country as a penniless labourer. I did all the dirty jobs there are. Dirtier jobs than just washing dishes, peeling potatoes and sweeping floors. But I was honest and worked hard. I sent money home to my mother, in Naples, while I still went around hungry myself. I made good. I want people to call me Sir Enrico.'

'Make it Sir Henry,' I suggested. 'It's easier for the Queen.'

'Right. Sir Henry, then. I want to hear the Master of Ceremonies announce loudly at a reception: "Sir Henry and Lady Salami".'

I rather liked Sir Henry for his outspoken simplicity.

He asked many more questions about the T.C.C. It was the Leo Doros Prize which caught his imagination. He inquired what sort of poet Leo Doros was. He was deeply touched when I described his great, deep love for birds.

'That's what I'm really interested in,' he said in the end. 'This Leo Doros Prize.'

'Surely, Enrico,' I told him, 'you can't give a hundred thousand pounds for this Leo Doros business?'

'Who's going to stop me?' he asked challengingly.

He sounded like Napoleon Bonaparte before Austerlitz.

LIGHTBROWN THURSDAYS

I

It was no empty threat either.

Enrico Salami gave his £100,000 to T.C.C. but Sam was equal to the occasion.

'If the money is given to the Leo Doros Prize, it will be spent on a Leo Doros Institute.'

'You can't spend a hundred thousand pounds on a Leo Doros Institute.'

'Can't I?' he asked with grim determination. 'We'll see. I'm going to build a Leo Doros Institute. In the hall there will be a bust of Leo Doros himself, by the best sculptor in Britain. By the best in the world.

'And why a bust?' he asked. But after some reflection he shook his head: 'No, it must be a bust. I think an equestrian statue of Leo Doros, with his sabre drawn and pointing skyward, would be going a shade too far.'

He looked tired, worn out and dispirited. I told him so.

'I don't like it at all,' he said. 'I used to be a happy-go-lucky man. I didn't have a worry in the world. Except that I had nothing to live on. But one can always find some kind of job. I had no responsibilities. I was unmarried then—so what did I care? I don't like this racket. I'm a fool to go on with it. But I'd be an even worse fool not to go on with it.'

'I know,' said I. 'You still hope to use the money for some really worthwhile . . .'

He interrupted me impatiently.

'Rubbish. . . That is self-deception. Rationalisation. If you live in a small flat, can't afford a car—what can you do with a car in New York, in any case?—and can't afford luxurious journeys—you don't really *miss* all these things. You forgo the whole lot cheerfully. But once you start living this sort of life, you are corrupted. I could not go back to my wretched little apartment in the Queens. I liked it then; I couldn't bear it now. I find even South Audley Street a little shabby and suburban on occasions. I am used now to flying all over the world on the slightest provocation and buying expensive and useless things. Durable goods they call them, I believe.'

'Cheer up, Sam,' I answered. 'I know that all rich men have a guilt complex and they try to feel miserable. You must bear your cross and go on living a life of luxury. I know it's hard on you; but you must be brave.'

'I am corrupted. I've lost my soul.'

'Don't be silly. People nowadays have no souls. Chekhov's heroes were the last people equipped with souls. After them, the thing has gone hopelessly out of fashion.'

'I haven't told you *all* my troubles,' he added gloomily.

'What are the rest?'

'Mariska.'

'Quarrelling again?'

'Oh no. I wish we were. Good old days, when we were still quarrelling. We love each other now. Dote on each other.'

'What's the trouble then?'

He sighed: '*Sholet*.'

That was a word I had not heard for many years, probably not since I left Hungary. *Sholet* was a dish of Polish-Jewish origin, but fairly popular with diverse layers of the population quite independent of race or creed. In fact, the *sholet* made in Uncle Stern's restaurant was the craze of Budapest for a while in the thirties. It is made of butter beans and large pieces of smoked pork (not the strictly orthodox one, of course) or goose, dripping with fat. It is one of the heaviest dishes ever invented by man, even by Polish Jews—not exactly the spiritual ancestors of light French cuisine. Cooking *sholet* is rather a complicated business: it has to be prepared twenty-four hours before being served and it has to be done in a really hot oven for a long time. People used to send it to the baker—only the baker's oven was really suitable. How Mariska solved her *sholet* problems in the Mayfair of London seemed a mystery to me; but apparently she had solved them somehow.

'She makes it twice a week. Sometimes three times. I can't go on like this much longer.'

'Why do you eat it then?' I asked.

The question seemed utterly incomprehensible to him.

'Why do I eat it? What else can I do with it?'

'Leave it.'

'Leave Mariska's *sholet*? Impossible. Do you remember Mucius Scaevola? The Roman gentleman who stuck his arm into the altar fire and let it burn to charcoal without blinking an eyelid? That was child's play. I could do it any day with a supercilious smile on my lips. But I should like to see the man who has the strength of character to push Mariska's *sholet* aside. I should like to see Mucius Scaevola facing Mariska's *sholet*.'

'He couldn't have pushed it away,' I told him, trying to stand up for Mucius Scaevola, 'because he had no arms left.'

'He had one arm left. Nevertheless, he couldn't have done it. Mucius Scaevola would have gobbled up Mariska's *sholet*, like the rest. Like myself.'

'That's suicidal,' I remarked.

'Of course it is,' he agreed. 'For a really passionate eater every meal is suicidal. Every dish of *sholet* is a nail in my coffin. A nail? A hook; a padlock; a grappling iron. But it doesn't matter: I prefer a pleasant death to a miserable life.' He shrugged his shoulders. 'Life itself is suicidal.'

'A gourmet like you . . .' I started to deliver a little sermon. But I got no further. He interrupted me:

'Don't be silly. I'm not a gourmet. A gourmet likes well-prepared, dainty dishes, sublime delicacies, while I eat heavy, disgusting stuff which would make any gourmet worthy of the name sick. A gourmet eats select food and, as a rule, very little of it; I devour vast quantities. A gourmet's plate is always empty; mine is always heaped. A gourmet eats slowly. I guzzle. Yesterday I finished two large calves' feet—*kalbshaxel*—before a proper gourmet could have had time to grind a little black pepper on his smoked salmon. No—*sholet* is no dish for gourmets, my friend: it's a lethal, self-destroying, quick-firing weapon. A gourmet's pleasure is an art of life; my gulosity is the art of death. An art of misery, in the best case. I'm no gourmet. Not even a gourmand. I am a gorger.'

2

By January 1956, preparations for the first Leo Doros prize-giving were far advanced. Sir Henry Salami had found a vast mansion in Westminster. It was a Victorian horror, built by one of the nineteenth-century merchant barons: a huddle of building around a vast, imposing and completely useless stair-case. The T.C.C. bought the house, Sir Seamus Cogg, R.A., made a bust of Leo Doros: the expression on Leo's face was meditative and his eyes seemed to look into eternity. Sam fixed the date of the prize-giving for early April and notified New York because Borsch, P. T. Trotter, Hazay-Hirschfeld, and a few others wanted to come over; and also Jocelyn Herb, the elderly short-story writer. And naturally, Mrs Leo Doros, the great man's widow, a focal point of these celebrations.

One day, early in February, it occurred to Sam that we had nobody to give the prize to. The T.C.C.'s Leo Doros Committee had been wildly busy; it was involved in strenuous and multifarious activities and was doing practically everything under the sun except the one thing it had been called into existence for: awarding the prize to a candidate.

Sam rang Borsch in New York to call attention to this point and he promised to ring back in a day or two and give the name of the winner.

'But there was no competition,' Sam objected.

'But there will be a winner,' Borsch reassured him, and after all that was the thing that mattered. Borsch kept his word and phoned next day.

'Listen . . .' he said. 'Hazay-Hirschfeld helped us out. He found a young American poet. A top talent, he says. Have you got a pencil and paper to jot her name down?'

'*Her* name?' Sam asked suspiciously.

'Yes. She's a young girl. Called Eleanor Sputz. I'll spell it for you: S-P-U-T-Z. The title of the winning poem is "The Frozen Magpie".'

'Sounds good.'

'It's beautiful. And very much in poor Leo's style. Miss Sputz is prepared to come to London in April.'

'But is she really good?' Sam asked anxiously. 'You're sure "The Frozen Magpie" is the goods?'

'Hazay-Hirschfeld says it's wonderful. I think so too. I nearly wept when I read it. Besides, we can't afford to be too fussy, can we? Well, goodbye, Sammy.'

I did not instantly recall where I had heard Miss Sputz's name before. As it *was* familiar I believed that I must have seen it in the pages of some literary magazine. But then, in a flash, the awful truth dawned on me: of course, she was my youthful editor from Allyears. How was it that Hazay-Hirschfeld, of all people, should recommend her for this honour, and with such suspicious warmth? I vaguely recalled that he had once been chasing some rare and expensive book on orchids ($120 net) and has asked me if I could help him. I had said I could not, but as Allyears were the publishers, I had given him Miss Sputz's name, saying that she might be able to trace a copy. I never heard the book mentioned again and had thought very little of Miss Sputz but, obviously, I had quite inadvertently laid the foundation of a blossoming friendship. I hoped it was a platonic one. It was too obscene to imagine anything else. Hazay-Hirschfeld was an old rogue of sixty-five and Miss Sputz looked about thirteen. The title, 'The Frozen Magpie', also sounded like one of Hazay-Hirschfeld's drearier jokes. Be that as it may, we were pleased to have a prize-winner at all. Miss Sputz was a presentable young lady even if she looked like a child prodigy. I only hoped that we should manage to keep the winning poem itself a well-guarded secret; it was unlikely, I thought, that the popular dailies would vie for its publication.

As soon as the name of the prize-winner became known, Ransome-Hall, who had so far collaborated with the scheme most enthusiastically, showed a great deal of antagonism and resentment. He had hoped, we suspected, to receive the prize himself. Now he made spiteful remarks about Miss Sputz and said he doubted her abilities. He announced that he would flatly refuse to print 'The Frozen Magpie' in *The Bridge*, which suited us perfectly.

But we needed Ransome-Hall's organising ability so Sam told him: 'Miss Sputz is a publisher, specially interested in poetry. So Matyas tells me. Perhaps she could be persuaded to print your *Lightbrown Thursdays*.'

This threw an entirely new light on the Sputz problem.

'Hm,' said Ransome-Hall thoughtfully. And off he went to visit Decimus Fox, our greatest living poet, to ask him to take part in the festivities and to deliver the Leo Doros Inaugural Lecture. We had really no hope of pulling this off; but Mr Decimus Fox accepted the invitation not only with his customary courtesy but with avidity. There was only one moment when he sounded a little doubtful.

'I know nothing of this man, Leo Doros. I have never heard his name before.'

'He was Hungarian, Mr Fox. A Hungarian poet,' said Ransome-Hall.

'That's true, of course. And I don't read Hungarian, do I?'

'I don't know, Mr Fox. With your many accomplishments . . .' replied Ransome-Hall with exquisite tact, spitting in Mr Fox's eye.

'No, I don't,' Mr Fox declared, wiping his eye sadly. 'But

the Hungarians are famous for their great poets. There was one called Vörös . . . Vörös-something.'

'Vörösmarty, I believe. That wasn't him.'

'Wasn't who?' asked Decimus Fox, perplexed.

'I mean Vörösmarty wasn't Leo Doros.'

'Then there was Ady,' he went on. 'A truly great poet, I gather. Would you say Ady was greater than Mr Doros?'

'I'd say Ady was greater. But Leo Doros was truly remarkable, too. Quite remarkable. If you have any doubts, why don't you ask MacKay?'

Mr Fox looked puzzled by this name.

'Of course you know Samuel MacKay, Mr Fox,' Ransome-Hall asked in a tone which implied that Mr Decimus Fox could not possibly be so ignorant as not to know Mr Samuel MacKay.

'I have heard of him . . . I can't say I have met him personally,' Mr Fox replied defensively.

Then he added, brightly: 'Indeed, yes.'

'Mr Jocelyn Herb will actually hand over the prize,' said Ransome-Hall slyly. 'If you are not in a position to accept, Mr Fox, perhaps we shall have to . . .'

There was no need to finish the sentence. Mr Decimus Fox accepted. He went on to ask Ransome-Hall what had happened to the three essays he had written for *The Bridge*. Ransome-Hall assured him that they were real masterpieces, and would soon appear. He commissioned three more essays and departed.

He was indeed an invaluable organiser. He collected a galaxy of splendid names in no time. For a while it seemed possible that the Prime Minister, Sir Anthony Eden, might be present at the opening of the Institute, but in the end we had to be content with a minor member of the Government. But Tony Ferdown was a Lord and the Americans were absolutely delighted.

'Is there anything between you and Miss Sputz?' I asked
Hazay-Hirschfeld sternly, as soon as I found myself alone
with him in the T.C.C. office, after his arrival in London. 'Is
there?'

'Of course not,' he protested hotly. 'What a filthy idea!'
He remained silent for a short while, then added: 'It is a filthy
idea which has been a dream of mine for quite a while. I don't
know why I denied the charge so indignantly. People always
do, I guess. If you are accused of something the other fellow
regards as a crime or sin, you protest vehemently. I ought to
have sighed nostalgically and answered in a dreamy voice:
"There isn't . . . ".'

'You are a dirty old man,' I told him with more moral indignation that I thought myself capable of.

'Indeed, I am. It's a new development. Until recently I
was a dirty middle-aged man. Before that a dirty young man.
Time, alas, refuses to stand still.'

He sighed.

'The overwhelming majority of men above, say, sixty-five,
are commonly labelled dirty old men. Why? Because they still
love doing something they can't do very well. My dear Matyas,
if everyone did only the things they can do well, this world
would be a different place.'

'Quite,' I agreed coolly, but I was already half converted to
his point of view.

'You needn't be jealous. All males are jealous of elderly
gentlemen and that is the cause of their moral indignation.
How silly. Half of the people over sixty-five are dirty old men
—and that is all there is to it.'

'It isn't. Why don't you follow the example of the other half?'

'Because the other half, my dear Matyas, the other half are
dirty old women.'

This point of general ethics having been settled, he continued: 'You seem to know little of the American female. Few of them are honest enough to go the whole hog. They love necking. Necking!' he repeated the word with contempt. 'Who is interested in necking? The neck is the only part of the female anatomy I have never been interested in. And I'm too old for *that* now. Besides, Eleanor having been brought up in the normal, idiotic way, and being as stupid as she is charming, she would be shocked if she knew that my interest in her is not purely platonic. Platonic? Oh no. Worse: purely paternal. So it has to be purely paternal. Damn it.'

Professor Hazay-Hirschfeld looked very prosperous. His scientific book-racket was booming and, he told me, he was often consulted nowadays, in an advisory capacity.

'I'm a very good adviser,' he assured me.

'On what?'

'On everything. It doesn't matter at all, on what. You are either a good adviser or a bad one. It has nothing to do with the subject; it's *advising* you have to be good at.'

'Nevertheless,' I insisted, 'the subject must come into it sooner or later.'

'Well—to a small extent, yes. It's like singing. Without having a trained voice, you cannot sing at all. If you do have a trained voice, you may be better at Schubert than at Wagner. Similarly, without a talent in *advising* you just can't advise. It's futile. But if you have a talent, I admit you may be better on certain subjects than on others. I personally find that if I really know something about a subject I'm never at my best. Knowledge somehow cramps my style.'

In a few days the Leo Doros festivities were in full swing. Many people arrived from America. I listened to many speeches, took part in innumerable cocktail parties, but it is mostly Sam I remember from those hectic days. For him, the festivities ended in disaster.

Sam and Ransome-Hall kept up a shuttle service between London Airport and the various hotels for quite a few days.

I went with them to meet Borsch, Mrs Leo Doros and P. T. Trotter, who arrived together. Borsch acted like the prodigal son of London, returning in triumph. Mrs Doros played the part of the great widow, aloof and disdainful. She had a nasty and disagreeable word for everyone, her most disgraceful and venomous sallies being reserved for the prize-winner, Miss Eleanor Sputz. Wilberforce S. Schmalz flew in with a host of other attorneys and worried Sam and Crispian to death by fussing about the details of the arrangements. He kept asking them if the invitations were all in order and if no one had been left out. Crispian told him repeatedly that he had first-class people for doing this job; everyone whose name figured in the records had been invited and brought over: there was no need for Schmalz to worry. Enrico Salami made an immediate hit with Earl F. Millington, the Ohio oil millionaire and his wife. Sam introduced them to each other and informed Earl that Enrico was on the verge of receiving a knighthood. Soon, he would be Sir Henry Salami, he added, to make his meaning quite clear. Earl F. Millington received this information with awe and enthusiasm.

'Gee. Fancy, Hazel, a Lord. A real Lord, this Sir Salami. That's what I like about British democracy. They make you a Lord in the end. That's kinda nice, don't you think so, Hazel?'

Hazel thought so and the Millingtons and the Salamis got on like a house on fire. Another person who made a smash hit with Earl F. Millington was Mariska. He regarded her as a great wit and repeated everything she said, choking with laughter. Mariska was uncertain at first whether this was an insult or a compliment but Sam convinced her that it *was* a compliment and, after that, she was flattered and pleased as Punch.

The Millingtons spent most of their time taking pictures, or more precisely, colour films. They searched out the famous London landmarks in order to produce documentary proof that they really had been there. He took guardsmen in front of Buckingham Palace from all possible angles, leaning into their mouths and crouching under their feet. The guards marched up and down as if unaware of Millington's presence. He worried poor Beefeaters in the Tower to death. He was particularly proud of a snap depicting Mrs Millington planting an innocent, if passionate, kiss on the lips of a Yeoman of the Guard. Mr Millington took Mrs Millington and then Mrs Millington took Mr Millington in front of the door of Number 10 Downing Street, and also on Westminster Bridge, with Big Ben in the background. But they refused to take each other in front of the Roosevelt statue in Grosvenor Square because 'that man' had been a subversive element and a dangerous Red. They photographed each other beaming in a taxi, parked in front of the House of Lords, standing over the white notice: FOR PEERS' CARS ONLY. It was only Mr Millington's age that prevented him from climbing the Nelson Column and having his picture taken, his arm thrown around the shoulders of the 'well-known British admiral'.

The last celebrity to arrive was Jocelyn Herb, the illustrious short-story writer. He was received by an array of photographers, television cameras and journalists. He made a statement to the Press:

'I am glad to be here and hand over the Eleanor Sputz Prize. I am especially glad to tell you that the winner, Mr Leo Doros, is an extremely able and pretty young lady.'

He quoted a few lines from one of his own distinguished and famous short stories and then he added how glad he was to be in Paris again, after so many years. When a rather inconsiderate television commentator pointed out that he had probably meant London, he laughed heartily.

'Of course I do. What a stupid mistake to make. In fact, I did see the Eiffel Tower when we flew in to land.'

Mr Herb had a wonderful Press, all the papers revived old anecdotes, recalled his great literary triumphs and masterpieces and added that in spite of his ninety-four years he had the mind of a schoolboy. Recalling the minds of some school-boys I know, that was probably true.

The actual celebrations went off without a hitch. Hazay-Hirschfeld had the happy idea of hiring a scooter to beat London traffic and he insisted on taking Miss Sputz to the Prize-giving on the pillion. She looked extremely pretty in a very tight frock which showed her thighs. The pictures taken at the moment of arrival were real cheese-cake and worthy of the widest possible publicity—which they duly received—although a literary caption was added in *The Times*. 'But she's got brains, too' said the *Mirror*'s caption, the picture itself showing practically everything else she had.

Before proceedings started, Wilberforce S. Schmalz had to be reassured once again by Sam that *everyone*, but really every-one, was there.

Decimus Fox made a magnificent speech, beating even his own personal record for the number of platitudes per minute.

'The predicament of poets,' he said in the course of his Leo Doros Inaugural Lecture, 'is said to be lack of faith. I wish to agree and disagree with these conclusions. Agree, because a lack of faith makes us hollow: disagree, because too much faith turns us dogmatic. The tragedy of our age is that aesthetic values do not keep pace with social—and, alas, technical—development. The challenge is to infuse living life into ancient traditions.'

He could go on like this for hours on end. And he did. He pointed out that the outstanding quality of Leo Doros's poetry was his humanity and added that 'paradoxically' his great love for animals was his most human trait of all.

Mrs Leo Doros nodded cool approval.

'Miss Eleanor Sputz's outstanding quality,' Decimus Fox concluded, 'is also her great humanity. The warmth of "The Frozen Magpie" is truly heart-warming.'

When Fox finished, Jocelyn Herb handed the prize—a small

silver statue of Leo Doros and a cheque for £1,000—first to Decimus Fox who handed it to Mrs Leo Doros who handed it to Miss Sputz.

The highbrow literary organs wrote leading articles on Decimus Fox's address, one entitled, 'A Crisis of Faith', and the other, 'A Challenge'. The photographers having, earlier in the proceedings, secured excellent pictures of Miss Sputz's upper thigh, were now keenly interested in a lovely young woman with long, blonde hair and a Madonna-face, occupying a seat immediately behind Mrs Leo Doros.

'Who is *she*?' asked a tabloid reporter.

Sam explained but the journalist did not quite catch his reply.

'That's quite a story,' he said with keen interest. 'Did you say she is the lift-girl for whom Leo Doros died?'

'I said nothing of the sort,' Sam snapped. '*For* whom he died? Brother, she's the lift-girl *on* whom he died. So, you see, there is no story in it.'

Having ascertained the identity of this most attractive young lady, Wilberforce S. Schmalz was easy in mind; it seemed that the list of invitations was, after all, pretty exhaustive. Having thus relaxed, he asked the blonde, Madonna-like lift-girl out for supper. She accepted.

Miss Sputz, in token of her gratitude to Crispian Ransome-Hall, took his book of poems, *Lightbrown Thursdays*, back to New York and succeeded in persuading Allyears to publish it. The book did appear in due course and sold eleven copies in the first six months, thus having a good chance of becoming the lowest-ever sale in American publishing history, narrowly beating the anti-Communist memoirs of an escaped North-Vietnamese prince, which sold twelve copies. Ransome-Hall was delighted to see his poems in book form in any case. After a long and hard struggle he managed to persuade the Executive Committee of the Trust for Christian Civilisation to buy four thousand copies of *Lightbrown Thursdays* for distribution among backward tribes in the Congo and Bechuanaland. So, in the end, everybody was happy—the T.C.C., Decimus Fox, Miss Sputz, Ransome-Hall, the backward tribes in the Congo and Bechuanaland, Mrs Leo Doros, Wilberforce S. Schmalz and the Madonna-faced lift-girl. Everybody was happy—except poor Sam.

4

I knew immediately that the *sholet* party was a silly idea but it never occurred to me *how* disastrous it might prove.

To crown the innumerable and endless procession of dinner and cocktail parties held, as a rule, in private suites in large hotels, Sam decided to have everyone in for a farewell dinner at his own place at South Audley Street. It was to be a *sholet* dinner in order to give Mariska a chance to shine.

'What d'you think of the idea?' he asked me with shining eyes.

'I think it's idiotic.'

'Do you?' He was disappointed.

'You just don't give *sholet* parties in London. Not everybody likes *sholet*.'

Had you informed a prince of the blood that some people are republicans, or an archbishop that some people do not believe in God, these pronouncements would have had a comparable effect. Not everyone liked *sholet*? Was I quite serious? Such people really existed?

'This *sholet* of yours is an acquired taste. If you like it, perhaps you love it; but if you don't like it, you most probably detest it. You can't inflict such a thing on your guests.'

It was absolutely useless and I knew it.

A day before the party I went to the food department of one of our large stores to help Sam with the shopping. We had instructions from Mariska to buy the drinks and a few tit-bits, green and black olives, cocktail onions and things like that, to be served with the apéritifs. Having selected the white and red wines and champagnes as well as bottles of gin, whisky, brandy and various liqueurs, we walked over to the food counters. There we saw a man in chef's garb, cutting smoked salmon with a long, thin knife. Sam stopped to watch him with ecstatic eyes.

'I must buy some smoked salmon,' he said in a blurred, strangely deep voice.

'Mariska told you not to buy anything that's not on the list.'

'But we need smoked salmon, too. For the little round sand-wiches, you know.'

He bought smoked salmon.

'Have you smoked sturgeon?' he asked the chef.

'The smoked sturgeon is very nice today, sir. Really beauti-ful,' said the latter in an enticing voice.

Sam bought smoked sturgeon.

He surveyed his surroundings. His eyes were glowing. He was enraptured and ravished; he was in the power of strange forces and there was no holding him back.

'Ham . . .' he whispered and his mouth watered. 'Smoked, Ardennes ham. Cut it thin as paper.'

He had by now forgotten his party and the tiny, round sand-wiches. He bought a cold duck; soused herrings; smoked trout; German and French sausages, from *knackwurst* to *andouillettes*; cold roast beef; jellied eel; artichokes; asparagus; prawns; and cheeses: Carré Frais, Camembert and Pont l'Evêque, Port Salut and Cantal, Fourmé d'Ambert, Bleu de l'Aveyron and Gex. I had stopped arguing with him: he was in a trance. He bought—the most mysterious of all his purchases—two dozen eggs. Then he bought gherkins: seeming to be fascinated by the way the man picked the dark-green, dripping pieces from the barrel with a long pair of wooden scissors, he bought more and more gherkins. He was breathing heavily.

'Anything else you require, sir?' asked the Mephistophelean chef.

'Nothing else,' came Sam's sulky answer. He looked tired, guilty and old.

Next day—the day of the party—I asked him what Mariska had to say about our shopping. I did not want to tease him; I was simply pleased to see that he had survived the storm and wondered how this came about.

'She never saw a thing,' said Sam gloomily. 'I intercepted the delivery man and told him to hide all the extra things and take them back. I told him to keep them as a present from me. I gave him ten shillings tip on top of it and pushed him out of the door. I thought he would go straight to the police—he was so flabbergasted and found it so strange—but apparently he did not. If I was a mad criminal—he must have thought—someone else should report me. He couldn't believe he had all that food—he was going to have the meal of his life.'

5

Sam's party was a great success and went off without a hitch. It was definitely Mariska's night. The *sholet* was a tremendous—although not universal—success. Most of the guests ate it avidly and praised it wildly: many of them were Central Europeans and thus experts. Wilberforce S. Schmalz was a true-born American but he appreciated good food when he saw it and made a pig of himself. It was Sir Henry Salami—for whom the dish was an entire and painful novelty—who contemplated the large beans and the gobbets of fat meat swimming in dark-brown sauce, with obvious, ill-disguised disgust.

'What is this?' he asked in an incredulous voice when he first set eye upon it.

'*Sholet*,' Hazay-Hirschfeld told him curtly. He did not like this question any more than an admirer of Brigitte Bardot likes answering an airy 'Who's this lady?'

Sir Henry Salami was a brave and enterprising man, otherwise he would not have reached his present station in the world. So he ate his *sholet* with admirable pertinacity but with an ever-darkening face. When he had swallowed his last bite, he threw his knife and fork down on the plate and turned to Hazay-Hirschfeld: 'Tell me, Professor: *as sholet*, is this good?'

Poor Lord Ferdown—the Parliamentary Private Secretary who had represented the Government at the opening of the Institute—was much too English to make any remarks. He suffered in silence, with that admirable courage which had built an Empire in the olden days and won many a famous battle on land and at sea. When asked, how he liked it, he said: 'It's very interesting. . . . Very interesting, indeed. . . .'

'Glad you like it,' said Sam and helped himself to another plateful. I thought it was the third.

Most of the others—including Miss Eleanor Sputz—raved about Mariska's masterpiece. Mrs Leo Doros the only person who refused even to touch it—threw contemptuous glances at Miss Sputz's plate and made some remark to the effect that a real poet should starve. One or two people nodded politely. Sam's reaction was to take more *sholet*.

'You can't make really good *sholet* in London,' Mariska remarked, fishing for compliments. 'Well, goose fat is not what it was in Kis-Harsany. Here they feed their geese on fish.'

Earl F. Millington roared with laughter at that.

'Feed geese on fish . . . Oh you sure are cute, Mariska. . . .'

Sam helped himself to another plateful. I began to frown, but he remained the charming and attentive host, showing no sign of strain. Mariska watched him with deep satisfaction. She drew me aside later in the evening: 'Tell me, Matyas, could Veronica cook at all?'

'Who?' I asked in astonishment.

'Veronica.'

'Who is Veronica?'

'Don't tell me you don't know. You're pulling my leg. Everybody is pulling my leg. She was Sam's first wife. You knew, I'm sure. Could she cook?'

Before I could tell her that I hadn't the slightest idea, Earl F. Millington parted us: he had been taking photographs, flashing bulbs into everybody's eyes and causing temporary blindness to many as well as a permanent stench affecting all.

'Come on, Mariska,' he shouted boisterously. 'We must have one together.'

He handed the camera to Schmalz and put a purple paper crown on his head and an orange-and-green one on Mariska's. (He always carried a few coloured paper crowns in his pocket just in case he needed them.)

'I'm a queen now,' said Mariska, laughing. 'Like Mrs Eisenhover . . .'

Earl F. Millington laughed at everything Mariska said but this he apparently regarded as quite a sensible remark. He stuck a funny paper hat on his wife's head, too.

'Earl has a wonderful sense of humour,' Mrs Millington told Sam, rather unhappily.

'Quite.' Sam nodded, and helped himself to another plateful.

'Curious thing *sholet*,' Borsch remarked. 'I like all things American; and all things English. But only Hungarian food. Patriotism is one thing; stomach-patriotism quite another.'

'American food is *beautiful*—beautiful to look at, I mean; Hungarian food is good. And in food, I for one, prefer taste to beauty,' said Sam and helped himself to more.

I could hardly believe my eyes. He looked sad but otherwise normal and at ease.

The guests left in high spirits. Earl F. Millington was still wearing his funny hat. And even Sir Henry Salami and Lord Ferdown had become reconciled with fate on tasting Mariska's Dobos and chocolate cakes. It was after one o'clock in the morning when the guests left. Sam showed them to their cars or, in one case, to their scooter, and ordered taxis for the others.

The party had been a great success.

At 3.30 Sam had a heart-attack and nearly died.

6

Three weeks later he was brought back to his flat from the nursing home. He was allowed to get up for a few hours every day. He had lost some weight but was cheerful and relaxed. He was not allowed to speak much; he tried hard to read but he tired quickly.

I went to see him on the day he came home and sat with him for a while, without speaking much. Dr Barna arrived, an ex-Hungarian who had been in London for twenty years, looking after a huge practice which consisted almost exclusively of well-to-do Hungarians and naturalised ex-Hungarians, with a few Germans, Austrians, Czechs and Poles thrown in. I do not think he knew what a sick Englishman looked like. He examined Sam with great care, checked his pulse, measured his blood pressure and listened to his heart.

'Show me your ankle,' he said. He pressed it. 'The other one.' Then he asked to see Mariska.

He talked to her in the entrance hall, just behind the door. Dr Barna, as a rule, preferred to speak bad English instead of good Hungarian, but this time—probably in order to be sure she understood—he addressed her in their common mother-tongue. He was adept at frightening his patients and their next-of-kin to death and he liked painting every picture three times darker than reality.

'Your husband is very ill, Mrs MacKay. He needs a great deal of rest and quiet, otherwise he will soon leave us. You know what I mean?'

Then, to dispel every shadow of doubt, he added: 'He'll die if he's worried too much, or if my instructions are not followed. He must not sit up more than three hours a day until I say so, which I think, I shall be able to do very soon. Eventually I want him to lead an active life—but not for the time being. But —you understand—until then, excitement of every kind must be carefully avoided if he is to survive.'

As this did not sound alarming enough, he went on: 'Which is by no means certain in any case.'

Mariska remained silent.

'You do understand, Mrs MacKay, don't you, that your husband is very gravely ill?'

'He'll be all right,' said Mariska.

'Yes—perhaps. But we must exercise the greatest care if we want to avoid a relapse and sudden death.'

He looked at her but there was no terror in Mariska's face, so he repeated it, even more glumly: 'There is a constant danger of sudden death and we can't be optimistic for some time to come.'

'Oh, he'll be all right,' she repeated, stubbornly.

'About food. This is of the utmost importance. I have given you my detailed instructions in writing. Don't give him any-thing—you understand—*anything at all* without referring to my list. You must use corn oil for your cooking. Animal fat is poison for him. It could kill him—make no mistake about that. Yes, it could kill him,' he repeated hopefully. 'You know exactly what to give him, Mrs MacKay?'

'Yes, I do.'

'He shouldn't put on weight. His weight is all right now.'

'He's too thin,' Mariska objected.

'He must not put on weight,' the doctor repeated strictly.

He left, moving out of the flat slowly, like a continental funeral horse. I felt he should have slowly nodding black feathers on his head.

Ten minutes later I said goodbye to Sam and went to the kitchen, to say goodbye to Mariska, too. She was frying two huge pork chops in goose fat.

'Is that for yourself?' I asked, taken aback.

'For both of us. Sam loves pork chops. He says I have a special way of making them.'

I gave no reply.

'Veronica could not cook. She could not even fry a pork chop,' she declared.

'Mariska,' I told her. 'You heard what Dr Barna told you.'

'What?'

'About dangerous animal fats.'

'Oh yes. . . .'

'Then why are you using them?'

'But this is goose fat. This isn't dangerous. This is the best goose fat there is.'

'But Mariska, my love, this is not a question of the quality of the goose fat. This is poison for him.'

'Goose fat? Poison? But it is very good for you. It's healthy. Dr Kondor knew a thing or two, too.'

'Who is Dr Kondor?'

'The doctor at Kis-Harsany. He was often called over even to Nagy-Harsany, he was so good. He said that goose fat was healthy. He told me that many times.'

'But Mariska, my angel . . .'

'He told me it was much purer than pork fat.'

'But, you see, this is not a question of purity. Medical science has found out a thing or two since you left Kis-Harsany. Don't you see . . .'

I stopped. It was no use.

'Sammy loves a good pork chop but only if it is fried in goose fat,' she said. 'I must fatten him up. He lost weight, poor Sammy. He needs nourishment. That's what you need after an illness.'

I looked at her sweet, honest, red face.

'Do you give him butter, too?'

'Sure. Plenty of butter. It makes him stronger.'

'But didn't you hear, Mariska,' I started again in despair, 'what Dr Barna said about animal fats?'

'But butter isn't animal. Butter is butter. You don't think of it as animal. Dr Kondor always said you had to eat plenty of butter after you've been sick. Gives your strength back. Sure it does.'

'Yes,' I said. 'It does.'

'I made arrangements with a Hungarian woman to send me goose-livers from Strasbourg. She lives there.'

'Very thoughtful of you,' I nodded. 'You did hear, didn't you, what Dr Barna said about sudden death?'

'Goose-liver gives you strength. And Sam likes it.'

'Oh, yes. I know he likes it.'

I strolled back to Sam's room. As soon as I got back I regretted it. What could I tell him? To look forward to an early death?

He looked at me. I looked at him.

He smiled: 'I told you once,' he said, 'that I'd rather die well than live wretchedly.'

I said nothing and left.

THE COUNT

In the autumn of 1956 I found myself in Belgrade, whither
Crispian Ransome-Hall had sent me to write a piece for
Bridge. He was in happy and triumphant mood; the appearance
of *Lightbrown Thursdays* meant a great deal to him. He showed
me the latest copy of *Peace and People* in which two of his
poems were reprinted.

'D'you think it's wise to appear in a periodical run by a
Communist front organisation?' I asked him.

'I don't care whether they are Communists, clerical reac-
tionaries or Buddhist priests. They publish my poems and my
poems are all right.'

'I wouldn't know.'

He asked me to write a long article on post-Canossa Belgrade.
He had in mind, of course, the visit of Khrushchev and Bulganin
to Tito the year before, when the two Russians were trying to
patch up the slight ideological misunderstanding that had
divided Stalin and the Marshal. It was obvious by now that
sundry new holes had appeared in the patch itself, so I accepted
my assignment with alacrity. From Belgrade I was to go on to
Sorrento, to join a horde of writers and university professors
in a conference convoked by the Trust for Christian Civilisation.
The theme of the conference was 'Europe, Asia and the Creative
Imagination' and it had no particular purpose, sense or reason.
The uninstructive phrase, 'creative imagination', being much
in vogue, had to come in, one way or another. But the basic
idea behind it all was a colossal spending spree dreamt up by
Sam some time before. Lots of people were invited from all
over Europe and Asia, their air-tickets and hotel bills paid for.
In return, they were to listen to four lectures daily on 'Europe,
Asia and the Creative Imagination'. The lecturers—who would

travel first class and stay in luxury hotels—would declare in various languages and on various levels of intelligence and articulateness that East and West had each a great deal to offer to the other and that they should seek to understand each other better, for the benefit of mankind. After the lectures the debate would be thrown open to the floor—i.e. to people who had flown tourist class and were put up in hotels with only four stars. They would repeat the same things all over again, some in halting English, others in fluent Korean—and there was one Laotian writer who would talk for hours in pidgin Cambodian. Simultaneous translation from and into three languages would be supplied at £325 per day. I told Sam that I wanted to spend about five days in Belgrade and then I would turn up at his conference.

'Convention,' he corrected me coolly. 'Not conference: convention.'

'What's the difference?'

'I'm not sure. But convention sounds far better. For all this money, I feel I ought to give the Trust a convention. Not a mere conference.'

I told Sam that talk about the 'creative imagination' rather exasperated me. There were only two phrases which nauseated me even more: the 'position of the intellectual' (in society and otherwise) and being 'committed'.

'Do you think they are committed? All of them?' I asked him anxiously.

Sam thought this over carefully: 'I don't know if they *are* committed . . . I shudder to think what some of them *have* committed.'

'Who is going to come over from New York?' I inquired.

'I fear the whole amiable lot—including the poet laureate and her aged beau. I hope Borsch will come, I rather like him. And I think P. T. Trotter and Earl F. Millington will honour us, too. I'm almost certain of them. But what can I do?'

He looked at me with some amusement: 'Do they put you off? Are you downhearted?'

'They would put me off in normal circumstances and I am downhearted in the extreme. But the attractions of Sorrento, the Bay of Naples and the chance of bathing in the Mediterranean outweigh their repulsion.'

I promised to go to Sorrento; I had every intention of going. It was no fault of mine that I never turned up.

Sam had put on a lot of weight. He was quite fat now but otherwise he seemed to be getting on well. He led an active life and although he complained of tiring quickly, I saw no sign of this. He tried to keep to some semblance of a diet but it was no use. His good intentions had little chance against Mariska's loving care coupled with his own love of food. I had the impression that he kept on doing everything he shouldn't, and flourished on it.

'About Belgrade . . .' he said before I left. 'My financial worries are solved for the time being. The Sorrento convention will get rid of a lot of unnecessary cash. Yet, money is still pouring in at a worrying rate. So it is the first duty of all of us to get rid of as much as we can. You've been rather slack lately, Matyas. Your expense accounts look amateurish.'

'What can I do? I hear the Danube is wide in Belgrade, of course I can always throw . . .'

He interrupted me sternly: 'Stop these childish jokes. I've heard them before. I've heard them much too often. The expense accounts must *look* right. You can't throw money into the Danube. That's what our patrons are doing but they must not be reminded of it by such crude methods. Spend on transport. Spend on hotels. Spend on entertainment. But spend, man! Don't throw! Spend!'

I started off with the best of intentions, but was not too successful. As I was driving down in my own car, I could not spend indefinite sums on transport. And Yugoslavia in those days was not a country where you could spend money. Nor was it a particularly gay place. I remember, as soon as I crossed the frontier, I sank into profound gloom. Between the Italian frontier and the outskirts of the first biggish town, Rijeka, I saw two hundred and fifty-six portraits of President Tito but only one motor car and three lorries. Every other village was celebrating something. I passed under a number of triumphal arches, bearing the legend: ZIVIO TITO. In the main streets of Rijeka loudspeakers were blaring. Someone was in the middle of making a stirring political speech but the towns-people did not seem to pay any attention whatsoever, neither did they seem to be troubled by the hullabaloo.

Poverty of the drabbest kind was universal but borne with great dignity. It was Communist poverty: everyone had his fair share of it. None of the revolting extremes of Southern Italy: no millionaires and starving beggars here. Communist poverty somehow looked juster, fairer, yet even more depressing and all-embracing.

For the first hour or so I felt inclined to turn back, but in a few days' time I grew to love these simple, sincere people. And because the generosity of the Serbs somehow permeated the air, even the English, American and other newspaper correspondents were kindlier and more helpful than anywhere else I had been. They made my work easy; they introduced me to people who gave me the information I needed; they brought numerous useful invitations. Almost all of them invited me to the International Press Club, partly because the food was very good there and partly because the head waiter was a Hungarian count.

Remembering Sam's stern admonition, for once in my life I was really determined to spend money lavishly, in fact foolishly. I decided to run up a bill in my hotel which would stagger him. The numerous invitations made my task harder but even with-out them—I was soon to realise—I was doomed to failure. Yugoslavia in 1956 was the cheapest country in Europe if not the world.

On my arrival I went to the Majestic—at that time the best hotel in the country—and asked for a suite.

'What exactly do you mean by a "suite"?' the receptionist inquired.

'Say two rooms. Or better, three. A bedroom and two sitting-rooms. And a bathroom, of course. With a balcony and a roof-garden.'

'We have no rooms. None at all.'

It turned out that a West German parliamentary delegation had just arrived and had taken all the rooms. The receptionist promised to do his best and when I got back three hours later, he informed me that he had succeeded in finding me a small room—without a bathroom. I was grateful. The price of my accommodation was eight and six a day.

Food, too, was heart-breakingly cheap. Drinks, including their ferocious plum-brandy, *slivovica*, were even cheaper. I went to interview, among other people, the editor of one of their national dailies. He told me: 'I must confess something. We have published some extracts from your book, *Horse Without Background*. We couldn't send you your fees because of the currency regulations. But now that you are here, we'll pay you.'

'No ...' I groaned. 'Don't ... No more money. Please ...'

'We must.'

'Have mercy,' I begged him.

'I'm sorry,' he shook his head. 'We must pay you. We couldn't send the money abroad but now that you are here you must have it.'

Suddenly I felt Sam's problem descending on my shoulders in miniature. You vainly pursue money all your life; and then, on some exceptional occasion, money starts pursuing you and there is no getting away from it. I knew I was not allowed to take dinars out of the country; in any case, they were practically worthless beyond the frontier. Now I had a room in Yugoslavia's best hotel for eight and six a day, was inundated with invitations for meals and parties, could find nothing at all to buy—there was simply nothing in the shops except some leather goods of which I had already bought far more than I needed—and now this kindly brute was offering me more cash! I admired their puritanical honesty; but I also felt irritated. I stuffed the thick wads of dinars I had just received from him into my pockets and felt disgusted by the inequities of life.

But I am not a man to lie down in vicissitude: I am a staunch, fighting spirit. I refused to be beaten by all that money pouring in or thrust upon me. Sam had talked about spending on travel, on hotel bills and entertainments. On the first two grounds I was defeated; but 'entertainment'—as understood by benevolent funds and tax offices—was still a promising possibility. A number of people had been kind to me so I decided to invite a full dozen of them to dinner for my last night in Belgrade. The International Press Club was the best place, so I'd been told, so the Press Club it was to be.

But first I had to visit the Press Club as a guest, not as host. As I had a few letters to write and as I wanted to see the English newspapers—all available there—I turned up an hour earlier than arranged. A boy of about fourteen wearing black trousers and a white jacket, approached me as I sat down at a desk to write my letters.

'Mr Matyas?'

'Yes.'

'I have a telegram for you.'

He went to fetch it.

It read: RING YOU TOMORROW EIGHTEEN THIRTY AT PRESS CLUB SAM MACKAY.

I put the telegram on the desk on the top of a pile of notes and other papers.

I had written about three sentences of my first letter when a tall man of rigidly aristocratic bearing entered the room. He looked at me coolly. It was an unpleasant, searching look. Then he said: '*Servus.*'

Now *servus* (or more precisely *szervusz*) is a Hungarian greeting with a curious semantic history. Although the word means 'servant' in Latin and the greeting in its full form means 'I'm your humble servant', its use became restricted to the middle and upper classes and it always implies social equality; indeed, it implies that you are on the familiar second-person

(German *du*) terms with the person you greet. No servant of yours would ever dare to greet you in this way, assuring you that he is indeed your humble servant. Its English equivalent would be something like 'Hallo, old chap' accompanied by a hefty slap on the back.

I looked at him with some surprise. As a waiter he would not dare to greet me in such fashion; as a Hungarian aristocrat of the old school he would not condescend to do so.

'You don't recognise me?' he asked me.

'I don't. But that doesn't mean a thing. I don't recognise anybody.'

He kept his unfriendly eye fixed on me and made no reply.

As he did not speak, I did: 'I've heard you were a count. You must have been a rather dissolute one if we met in Budapest. The only members of the aristocracy I knew were the black sheep who had sunk to becoming actors, journalists, play-boys and prize-fighters. Or the worse ones who married actresses and chorus girls. The ones who spent their lives riding, shooting, hunting, fishing and gambling, were far above my station.'

He smiled for the first time.

'You're right. Let's say you're almost right. I was an actor.'

'Why "almost" right then? I was right.'

'No, only almost right. Because I wasn't a count either. Ever heard the name Schwarz?'

You might as well ask an Englishman if he has heard the name Smith or a Frenchman if he's ever met someone called Dupont. Yet, common as his name was, he had rung a bell.

'You're not Jonathan Schwarz by any chance?'

'I am.' Then he added anxiously: 'For God's sake, don't give me away. My job here depends on being a haughty member of the Hungarian aristocracy.'

'I won't give you away. But I can hardly believe that . . .'

He interrupted me nervously.

'Don't be foolish. They'd be so disappointed I'd probably

122

lose my job. You know that the most ardent supporters of the British monarchy are the republicans of France and the United States. You know how in Britain Trade Union leaders, having spent a lifetime fighting against privilege, have only one real ambition: to get a knighthood or, preferably, a peerage. When others get a barony, that's "privilege"; when they get it, they are just doing their duty by strengthening the Socialist opposition in the House of Lords. Similarly, I assure you, the Communists love titles and rank almost as much as those rabid British Socialists. They are mad about titles. They made a great hue and cry about abolishing titles. Even that is untrue. They abolished the old titles and created new ones. But they are terrible snobs and don't really think very much of the new titles. My claim to distinction here is that I'm a count.'

'Except that you aren't.'

'Yes. That's a snag. But I treat them with aristocratic contempt. That's what they insist on. That's what they pay me for. As long as I look down on them, they are quite prepared to look up to me. It is as simple as that.'

'But how did they come to take you for a count in the first place?'

'Well, you see, my stage name used to be Andrassy and they assumed that I was a real Andrassy. And I . . . how shall I put it . . . did not discourage them in their belief.'

I remembered the young country boy who joined our school in Budapest when I was about fifteen. He was shy, timid, retiring and spoke with a funny Northern—almost Slovak—accent. He was the butt of innumerable cruel pranks and, as though to give us every reason to dislike him still more, he soon became by far the best scholar in our form. We detested all good scholars who took their studies seriously: only a natural brilliance was forgivable. One could become top boy if one could not help it; but this newcomer, Stephen Schwarz was *trying*. Yet, in spite of all these shortcomings, he was soon surrounded with a great deal of admiration and envious interest, because of his elder brother, Jonathan—whom we occasionally saw and hero-worshipped in the corridors. Jonathan was everything Stephen was not. He drank; he chased women, he played cards; he regularly failed in Latin and mathematics. His exploits filled us with awe and admiration. He reached the pinnacle of fame when, one morning, he arrived at school straight from a night club of ill repute, still wearing his dinner jacket. He was expelled because of this and we never saw him again. But we occasionally heard of him, when he hit the headlines. Once he was accused of having forged his rich landowner father's signature on a promissory note, but was acquitted. Whether his father accepted his forged signature as genuine to save his son, or someone else had forged his signature in the first place (as was suggested at the trial), I do not know. Although he was acquitted, the public always referred to him from that time onwards as 'that clever forger'. (*Clever*, because he had been acquitted.) Eventually Jonathan became an actor and a very unsuccessful actor at that. He looked wonderful—he was tall, slender and aristocratic, while his brother, Stephen, was short and plump with strong Semitic features. Although he took the aristocratic name Andrassy, he usually played butlers, waiters or coachmen whose part was limited to announcing the arrival of a visitor or informing those on stage that dinner was served.

My hosts arrived at the Press Club and we spent a long and pleasant evening. We listened in to every news bulletin on the Club's radio in Serbo-Croat, Hungarian and English; strange and exciting news kept pouring in from Poland. Gomulka seemed to have defied Khrushchev and Khrushchev seemed to have accepted defeat. Curious, we thought. And still more curious news arrived about tension and agitation in Budapest. When, at last, I was about to leave, the Count—as everyone called him—reappeared.

'You know Sam MacKay, do you?' he asked and handed me back Sam's telegram, which I had left on the desk.

'Do *you* know him?'

To this he did not give a straight answer but made a very

peculiar remark: 'So he sends telegrams nowadays, does he? Little wonder that he is not keen on sending registered letters.'

This was so utterly senseless that, I decided, it was bound to have some deeper meaning. But the Count offered no explanation.

'Sam's father,' he said, 'was the vet in Bagocz, the village where my father was a landowner. I knew Sam from childhood. We played football together when I was five.'

'And you remained friends.'

'Oh, no. Not really. We lost contact.' He hesitated. 'Not completely though.'

He stopped again.

'Except, you see, that I was cited as a co-respondent at his divorce.'

'I see . . . So *you* were the co-respondent.'

'No, I wasn't. Not *the* co-respondent. I was one of the co-respondents.'

He looked at me quizzically: 'You mean to say you don't know the story?'

'I don't,' I replied.

I told the others I was staying behind with the Count. We went back and sat down at our table, he ordered some good Yugoslav Riesling—of course I did not dream of not accepting his hospitality—and while lighting one cigarette from the stub of another, he began to speak.

2

'I don't think I've ever seen a more wonderful woman than Veronica Toth,' the Count began. 'If one went into detail, it could probably be said that her face was not too regular; that her nose was not straight; that she opened her mouth too wide when she laughed. No doubt. But all in all, taken as a human being—no, no, not as a human being, as a woman—there was just no one to come near her. First of all, she was a redhead, and her wonderful red hair made her the centre of attention everywhere she went. She was tall; she was always gay; she was witty; she was cruel; she was kind. She wore her beauty with a simple, natural pride but without conceit. To be with her was exciting, amusing and exasperating.'

'You sound as if you were in love with her.'

'As if? . . . Man, what do you mean by "as if"? I was mad about her. I was crazily and hopelessly in love with her. And so was the whole village of Bagocz.'

'With one or two possible exceptions,' I interjected.

'If there were exceptions I was not aware of them,' he retorted dryly. 'When she came down to spend the summer with Dr Arpad Toth, her uncle, the physician, the whole village fell for her: the boisterous ladykiller, the owner of the timber yard, all the army officers within a radius of twenty kilometres, all the civil servants, all the rich and all the poor, old and young alike. The dentist from the neighbouring village serenaded her with a gipsy band every single night throughout the summer—seventy-three times all told. Katona, the grocer, quarrelled with his wife on account of her—resenting her by no means unjustified jealousy—and beat her up after twenty-four years of matrimonial bliss. Bato, a young clerk in the district court, started drinking because of her and died of delirium tremens two years ago. I too was in love with her. So was my shy little brother, Stephen. And so was Sam. He wasn't much of a conformist but, you see, it was practically impossible not to be in love with Veronica Toth.'

'And whom did *she* love?'

'All of us. She flirted with us all, teased us all—but no one more than the next man. In spite of her come-hitherish manner she was really unapproachable. And as there were always too many people around her—her admirers saw to it that no one should be left *à deux* with her—there wasn't really much opportunity for anyone to "approach" her. She loved us as a crowd; individually we were country bumpkins for her. She loved her group of admirers, but took no individual seriously. She was enjoying herself.

'We weren't jealous of one another. Well, perhaps just a little. But jealousy didn't really come into it. She was a supra-natural phenomenon. One is not jealous of the sun for shining on others, too. In the end, loving Veronica wasn't really love; it was a religion. The religion of the Bagocz male.'

'This is all very colourful,' I told him. 'But aren't you exaggerating just a little?'

'Not at all. Loving Veronica Toth was a mass hysteria. Something like panic gripped us when we remembered that she would have to leave us soon. Not because she was going to leave A or B, mind you; but leave *us*, as a community. None of us had a shadow of a chance at Bagocz; but we knew we'd all have still less of a chance once she went back to Budapest. That is to say less than nothing. Well, minus three is less than zero.'

'Does mathematics come into it, too?'

'In a minor part only. When I went back to school in Buda-pest I never dreamt of looking for her. Why should I? Surely, we could not hope to rival the dandies and wits of the capital. Modesty was never one of my most outstanding virtues but even I had to accept facts which stared me in the face. I don't say that adoration of Veronica Toth was quite as widespread in Budapest as in Bagocz, but it seemed pretty widespread. I ran into her occasionally. Once I saw her dancing at the skating rink in the City Park, on the Big Lake. Then I saw her among the opening couples at the Jurists' ball. She looked like a goddess with that red hair of hers and she danced the *csardas* superbly. I didn't even ask her for a dance. What for? She had admirers galore without me ... I had heard that she had turned down scores of suitors: sons of counts and barons, sons of rich industrialists and rich industrialists themselves; officers and politicians. Then suddenly—about three weeks after the Jurists' ball—I heard that she had married Sam Makkai.

'You could have knocked me down with a feather. I recalled

that I had seen Sam at the ball. They had danced together. All I thought was: what a fool Sam is to chase unattainable dreams, and I dismissed the matter from my mind. What an odd choice this was. Sam wasn't good-looking; he wasn't rich; he wasn't dashing and flamboyant; he wasn't even particularly intelligent. He certainly was not much in comparison with some of Veronica's suitors. Perhaps it was just bravado on her part. She did it *pour épater le bourgeoisie*. Well, whatever the reason may have been, she did marry Sam. And she did astonish the world. She certainly astonished me.

'As soon as we—the world and I—recovered from our surprise, we said it wouldn't last. But we had no idea *how* short it would be and how disastrously it would end. The only reason that the marriage lasted for some years—nominally, at least—was that war broke out and the two of them were separated for long intervals. The marriage dragged on till after the war, when the Communists took over. Veronica's former counts and barons ceased to be counts and barons. (I am the only person to be elevated to the peerage in the Communist world, but that happened later.) At the same time, Sam got quite a good job in one of the ministries. But even this failed to improve matters.

'There were two main difficulties, I thought. The first was that once Veronica *had* impressed the world, had astonished the bourgeoisie and all Budapest society with her odd choice, and had now got over the thrill that gave her: she was bored to tears by Sam. Sam was too nice for her; too romantic, too adoring, too gentle, too eager to please, too obedient. She teased him, tormented him, despised him. And she was unfaithful to him.

'And that was the second trouble. I think Veronica was a virgin when she married. I know this may sound a bit old-fashioned, even incredible, but virgins do exist and I am sure she was too proud to permit any male to "possess" her—as the saying goes. She refused to be "conquered". But once she tasted it . . . well, it's a curious story . . . She started having innumerable affairs—quite a few scandalous ones. Everyone knew about them except . . . well, guess who. Why did she behave so? I can offer many complex explanations, using the full vocabulary of psycho-analysis. They may be right. I don't know. Personally I'm a simple soul. Perhaps there was in all this an element of revenge on Sam: he had to be punished for *her* mistake, but she did it mostly—childishly simple though this may sound—because she liked it. She just enjoyed a good . . . you know what. She just loved it. Passionately. Passionately, I think, is the right word.

'Some of her affairs were in the worst possible taste. And she did little to conceal them. In fact, she did everything to advertise them. So eventually even Sam was bound to pick up some of the rumours. First he dismissed them as too mean and base to be worthy of notice. But they persisted, there were too many anonymous letters, oblique "friendly" warnings, queer looks, whispers and giggles behind his back, and he had to do something. So he charged Veronica—not with infidelity, he never really believed that—but with indiscretion. She must have behaved foolishly to give rise to all this gossip. Veronica grew irritable and annoyed. Her keen disappointment, all her missed opportunities, all her frustrated dreams flashed up in her mind—and now this dull little man, the cause of all her misery, dared to accuse *her*. She laughed at him. She admitted that she had been unfaithful. There was a frightful row but Sam did not really believe her. He was sure that she only meant to torment him. "Name your lover!" he shouted at her. "Name my lover?" she laughed. "Very well." She sat down, took up a pencil and jotted down a list. There were twenty-four names on it.'

The Count emptied his wine glass: 'I was one of them. One of the twenty-four.'

Then, after a brief pause: 'In fact, I was number seventeen.'

I could not decide whether this was meant to sound romantic or bashful. But I did not dwell upon this problem.

He continued: 'Sam left the house and in his first fury and humiliation he ran to a friend of his, a lawyer, and instructed him to start divorce proceedings and cite twenty-four corespondents. He handed over the list, in Veronica's handwriting. The lawyer called in his secretary and dictated a letter to Veronica, informing her of Sam's decision. He told the secretary to send this letter by registered post.'

I pricked up my ears at the words 'registered post'. Hadn't he said something most peculiar about registered letters?

'Sam spent half the night drinking—a very rare indulgence in his case—the other half walking on the bank of the Danube and in the hills of Buda. By 3 a.m. he decided that he had acted rashly and found a number of excuses for forgiving Veronica, whom he adored; the first and main excuse being that she had been joking in any case and had never been unfaithful. He made up his mind to intercept the post next morning but that was difficult in the case of a registered letter addressed to Mrs Makkai—Central European post offices are not as casual about such matters as the British. He decided to do the next best thing: perhaps the letter, after all, should be delivered. Veronica clearly needed a shock and a warning. But he would, he decided, appear in the flat a few minutes after the letter, explain everything, forgive her with a grand and magnanimous gesture and end up with a great act of reconciliation, in bed.

'After that sleepless night, he turned up very early in front of his house. He waited an hour and a half. At last, he caught sight of the postman who had stopped to chat with a young woman around the corner. When they parted, the postman helped a little girl—a small child going to school particularly early for some reason—to cross the road. Sam went up to his own floor and stepped behind the door leading to the back stairs. A few more minutes and the postman arrived. He rang the bell. No one answered. He rang again. Still no answer. Cold sweat poured down Sam's face: "She didn't spend the night at home" he thought. But at last a sleepy Veronica opened the door—Sam just caught a glimpse of the red hair. He also noticed that she was wearing the thinnest of nightdresses—no dressing gown. She said something to the postman. Then she signed that book they carry along with them for registered letters, but still they went on talking. Sam saw her smile. Then suddenly the postman pushed the door open, skipped into the flat and slammed the door hurriedly behind him.

'Ten minutes later a dishevelled postman, red in the face, reappeared with his big, black bag on his shoulder and a bunch of letters in his hand. He looked a bit dreamy; he started off on his round whistling.

'Sam left the house. Later that morning he rang his lawyer and told him to proceed with the case. Then he disappeared— no one heard anything of him for three weeks or so. His un-explained absence cost him his job at the ministry. But, of course, he did not care. Eventually he turned up, had a quiet, even sub-dued, interview with Veronica in her lawyer's office and asked her to divorce him. Veronica said that she did not care either way but she saw no reason for not fulfilling Sam's request. So they were divorced—the reason being Sam's own admitted adultery. After that Sam applied for a passport—this was still possible in early 1948—and left the country. And that's why and how the United States of America gained such a splendid new citizen.'

That was the end of the Count's narrative.

'How do you know all these details about the postman?' I asked him. 'It must have been a secret, known only to three people.'

'Secret? A secret of this kind in Budapest?... Don't be silly, Matyas. You were born and bred in the city—you ought to know better. I could think of twenty-five different explana-tions, but I won't bother. I shouldn't put it past Sam's lawyer to spread such a juicy bit of gossip. Professional secrets are kept in Budapest only when they are too dull to be told. I don't know how it all came out; but out it came.'

I could not argue with the Count. I knew my Budapest.

'Everybody knew this story in Budapest. People laughed their heads off. People always laugh at tragedies and shed tears over the idiotic plight undeserving fools get themselves into.'

He poured out some more wine.

131

'Having said so much, I'll add two more details. Perhaps unimportant; nevertheless, parts of the story. After Sam's departure, Veronica led an irreproachable life. Chaste, I mean. Irreproachable is perhaps not the right word for it; I reproached her often enough. So did many others. But it was of no avail. The golden youth of Budapest—I among them—hoped that the lovely Veronica would be their fair prey. But there was nothing doing. Perhaps she was ashamed of herself. Perhaps she had had enough. I don't know. She was unpredictable. She became as aloof, remote and unconquerable as she had been in her maiden years.'

The Count fell silent.

'And the other minor detail?' I prompted him.

'Oh yes. I may be quite wrong in that; ridiculously wrong perhaps. But I had a feeling that she still loved Sam. *Still?* No: now, slowly, she grew to love him. I couldn't tell you why ... Or perhaps I could. Sam was the only person who'd ever appreciated her as a human being *and* a woman. She never wanted to be treated just as a lovely redhead—she resented that. It's a common enough attitude in beautiful women. But Veronica would not permit anyone to forget, either, that she was a beautiful woman. Certainly she wanted a lover, not a grandfather. Not just a friend. But I'm sure what she really wanted was a lover *and* a friend. With Sam she could talk between embraces; and he could make love to her between intellectual chats. Many men loved her; Sam was the only one who also liked her. So, as soon as he was out of sight, he grew in stature and became a faraway, legendary figure in a distant land. Slowly she forgave him all his kindness; all his softness and gentleness; all his devotion to her. She forgave him all his virtues and became his faithful and dutiful wife—once she had ceased to be his wife and as soon as seven thousand kilometres divided them from each other.'

'Quite a romantic story,' said I. 'In spite of the registered letter.'

'It *is* a romantic story,' the Count replied with some fierceness

132

in his voice. 'And I won't have any cheap, cynical jokes about it.'

It was half past two in the morning. I was about to leave, at last, when the Club was suddenly invaded by a number of correspondents. My former host returned too—this time without his wife. Revolution had broken out in Hungary and the newspapermen had work to do. Yugoslavia was a key point —all the world wanted to know Belgrade's reaction. The Hungarian Party Secretary, who had just returned from Belgrade, by the way, had called in Russian tanks to quell the 'riot'; there was shooting in the streets of Budapest. Tumultuous chatter and hunger for more news kept us up all the night. Vast numbers of cups of black coffee were consumed; and even more glasses of whisky and soda. Tense groups gathered round the ticker tape machines and many theories and prophecies were propounded.

Next evening Sam rang me at the time indicated in his telegram. 'Well, Matyas,' said he, 'everything has changed now. What I originally wanted was . . . well, never mind. That's past history. What I want *today* is that you should go to Budapest as soon as you can and write a damn good report for the *Bridge*.'

'I have no visa.'

'Don't talk to me about visas. Go to Budapest. The rest is your affair. Oh, and one more thing . . .'

'Yes. What is it?'

He swallowed audibly but still sounded casual: 'One more thing. Bring my wife out with you. My ex-wife, I mean. Not Mariska. She's here all right.'

'Do you know her address?'

'No. Find her. Goodbye.'

Twenty minutes later Sorrento phoned again. This time it was Crispian Ransome-Hall asking me to wait for him—he would turn up in Belgrade as soon as possible—and we would be going to Budapest together.

Even the exhilarating and wildly exciting events across the
border did not make me forget my duty to get rid of as much
money as possible on hehalf of the T.C.C. As I had to wait for
Crispian in any case, there was no need to cancel my banquet for
twelve. In the morning an English friend, a radio correspondent,
rang me up. He sounded very diffident and finally made me
promise that I would give a frank answer to his most straightforward question. I promised. Well, fresh lobster had arrived
in the Press Club—a great delicacy but an even greater rarity
in those parts. Could they order some for dinner?—because
unless ordered it disappeared in no time. Fresh lobster was
very expensive—he added—but as we were friends, he hoped
I wouldn't mind if he and the others offered to contribute
something towards my expenses. I assured him that contributions were out of the question. I rang the Press Club, asked
the Count to keep some lobster for all of us as a first course;
this to be followed by steak, and the steak by chicken.

My dinner was a great success. We consumed that huge
repast—the lot of it—in high spirits, amid animated chatter.
White wine was followed by red, red wine by champagne,
brandy and liqueurs galore. My thoughts took me to the streets
of Budapest. To the freedom fighters. And to Veronica Makkai.
Nevertheless, I was able to spare a trivial thought for my
splendid success in squandering T.C.C. dollars.

I asked for the bill and it came with a sobering shock. The
whole sumptuous dinner party for twelve people, with lobster,
steak and chicken, with champagne and all, cost me the equivalent of eight pounds, six shillings and threepence. I felt not
only frustrated but cheated. I made an angry protest. When the
Count at last understood that I found the total too little and
not too much, he laughed aloud.

'But this Press Club is a specially cheap place even in this
cheap country. Cheap for you, I mean; it's expensive enough
for us who live here. Didn't you know that it is heavily subsi-

dised by the government? They want to keep on the right side of the foreign Press.'

'But what the hell is this extra ten per cent? Surely, this should be *added* to the bill. Not *deducted*, man!'

'That's an extra ten per cent discount. To my personal friends.'

'You can't . . . Jonathan; really, you can't. That's the limit. You must add that ten per cent. And add twenty-five per cent for service.'

'Impossible,' he said coolly. 'All my friends get a discount. You *are* my friend, aren't you? . . . And as far as a tip is concerned . . .' he said this superciliously, 'I'm not in the habit of accepting tips from my friends.'

'No, no, not you. But there were others . . . Perhaps they might condescend . . .'

'That's all right,' he said in an icy tone and it sounded very final.

It's no good fighting your fate.

Luck and money may pursue you as relentlessly as misfortune.

I paid my eight pounds six shillings and threepence.

Next morning Crispian Ransome-Hall arrived. We jumped into my car and drove off towards the Hungarian frontier.

VERONICA

The Yugoslav frontier guards shook hands with me and wished
me luck. They advised me to get out of the car and cross the
small stretch of no-man's-land to the Hungarian frontier post
on foot. I followed their advice, wondering what it would feel
like to face these notorious AVO monsters for the first time in my
life. I knew that the AVO—the Communist Gestapo—wore
Russian-type uniforms with blue insignia on their collars. The
frontier branch, however, had green insignia. This was, literally,
the only difference between the two branches. Otherwise they
vied with each other in thuggery and sadism—many of them
were former Nazis. This is not surprising. The Hungarian
equivalent of the Gestapo, and the AVO, were both recruited
from the criminal underworld, and a small country like Hungary
cannot supply more than one set of these malignant psycho-
paths. Communists and Nazis must perforce use the same
recruits.

I decided to cut a cool and dignified figure as I faced my first
AVO man. I was, after all, a foreign visitor, with a British passport in my pocket.

So I strolled towards the AVO hut at my coolest and most
dignified. Suddenly a bullet whizzed past my ear. When I say
'past my ear' I am aiming at strong dramatic effect. It must
have been at least fifty yards away. But even that was near
enough for me. A second and a third bullet followed almost
immediately. A voice shouted from nowhere: 'Run, you fool!
They'll kill you.'

I threw dignity to the winds and rushed towards the AVO
post as fast as my feet could carry me. More shots rang out
before I could reach it, so I lay down flat in the grass. Suddenly

I noticed a peasant youth sitting under a tree, eating a piece of bread, and cutting alternate slices from a chunk of paprika *speck* and a large green pepper, with a big clasp-knife. He was the picture of unconcern. He looked eternal: one would have said he'd sat under that tree for thousands of years and would remain there to the end of time. It must have been he who had shouted at me. 'What's going on here?' I asked. 'The AVO?'

'Yeah . . .' he replied with his mouth full. 'The AVO.'

'Who are they shooting at?'

He swallowed a large chunk of *speck* and then asked me quietly: 'Who?'

'What d'you mean "who?"? I mean: Who are the AVO shooting at?'

'No one,' he said, thrusting his knife into a piece of *speck* again and manœuvring it into his mouth.

I remembered: nothing made me lose my temper so much as the imperturbable calm of the Hungarian peasant.

'Well, who is shooting at whom then?'

'People are shooting at the AVO,' he said.

'I see,' I said. I wasn't sure that I did see.

'There's a revolt going on,' he informed me. 'They're hanging the bastards on trees. High time, too.'

He grinned with delight.

I know I ought to have said—sternly if possible—that this was all wrong; that no one, not even the AVO, should be executed without a proper trial. But I am afraid I just grinned myself, too.

'That's why they are trying to get over the border. But there are some chaps over there, beyond that hillock, after them.'

Having said this, he concentrated again on his *speck* and green pepper. I could see no chaps and no AVO men round the hillock. I did hope, in any case, that the AVO men from the hut had already fled, and that Crispian and I would be able to cross the border without let or hindrance.

The shooting subsided and I walked to the hut. I knocked on the door which was opened immediately. I stood face to face with the AVO man: the first thing that caught my attention was the green insignia on his collar. Of course, it was silly to expect a monster; but it was surprising to find a pleasant-looking peasant of about twenty-five, with a round face.

I greeted him in Hungarian.

'My friend and I wish to cross into Hungary,' I told him.

'Certainly,' he replied. 'May I see your passport?'

I handed it over. He sat down at his tiny desk and started turning the pages over with his stubby fingers.

'Where's your Hungarian visa?' he asked.

'I haven't got one.'

He looked at me with shifty, cunning, suspicious eyes.

'I cannot let you in without a visa.' He was polite but sounded dreadfully final.

'There's a revolution going on,' I argued. 'Surely in these extraordinary circumstances . . .'

He interrupted me.

'I don't know anything about extraordinary circumstances,' and he looked at me with those unpleasant, penetrating eyes. 'I have received no instructions from my superiors to let anyone in without a visa.'

He stood there—prickly and unsmiling—and handed back my passport.

What were those shots outside? I asked myself. This doesn't look like the AVO in full flight.

'I heard some shooting when I was coming here,' I said cautiously.

'Yes?'

'Is it true that revolutionaries are hunting AVO men?' I asked, perhaps not too subtly but I thought I had nothing to ose.

'Quite true,' he nodded. 'The *blue* AVO.'

So that was the new line. The blue AVO—the political police

in the stricter sense of the word—were the villains, but the green AVO who patrolled the Iron Curtain, shot at refugees, blew their legs off with mines and tortured them when caught, were our little brothers, decent fellows, progressive intellectuals, almost supporters of the revolution.

A lorry stopped outside the hut. Seven or eight men in civilian clothes, wearing revolutionary armbands and carrying rifles, jumped down. These must be the freedom fighters, I thought, who were shooting at the AVO men. We'll see, I said to myself with malicious anticipation, whether they, too, recognise these fine distinctions between the blue AVO and the green AVO. Perhaps they will hang him on a tree—in complete disregard of the greenness of his insignia. In which case Crispian and I might be able to proceed.

'Hullo, Johnnie,' said the leader of the revolutionaries to the AVO man.

'Hullo, Toni,' the policeman replied amiably.

'Cigarette?' and the leader of the revolutionaries offered him one from a silver case. 'Nice to see you again.'

'How are things in town?'

'Fine. Fine,' replied the leader of the revolutionaries. 'We've got the town pretty well in our hands. The Communist leaders are mostly staying indoors. A sort of house arrest, although nobody really calls it that. Eight of them are in jail.'

'So the town is in your hands?' said the political policeman. 'Glad to hear it. That's good news.'

'Not much bloodshed,' added the leader.

'Thank God for that . . .' murmured one of the revolutionaries.

The AVO man nodded emphatically as though violence were the one thing he abhorred.

'They hanged three AVO men. That's all.'

'Two on trees, one on a lamp post,' explained a little fat man, obviously given to minor detail.

'They were all blue AVO, I suppose,' remarked the AVO man peevishly.

'Of course,' nodded the leader of the revolutionaries.

'Of course, Johnnie boy,' nodded the small fat man, too.

'Who is this chap?' asked the leader, turning towards me.

'My name is Matyas. I'm a Hungarian writer, living in London.'

'Matyas? . . . But you can't be the Matyas who wrote *Horse Without Background*!'

'The very man.'

'Oh boy . . . That's a bit of luck for us. What are you doing here?'

'I'm trying to get to Budapest with an English friend of mine. He's a very well-known journalist. Editor of the *Bridge*—you must have heard of it.'

I said this in a tone which implied that only an idiot and a boor had not heard of the *Bridge*. I breathed not a word about our successful propaganda campaign which had almost managed to bring the number of our subscribers up to five hundred.

'You don't say . . . the *Bridge*?' said the leader.

'You mean he's personally here? The editor of the *Bridge*?'

'Waiting over the other side.'

'But what are you wasting your time here for, then? Why don't you go? . . . You're not trying to keep them out, Johnnie boy, are you?'

As all the eight men were carrying guns, I felt reasonably confident that Johnnie boy would be accommodating. He smiled politely but his eyes flashed at me with anger: 'To Budapest? . . . You never told me you wanted to go to Budapest.'

'I'm sorry. I must have forgotten.'

'You should have let him in,' said the leader sternly.

'I thought he wanted to go to Baja,' he said fixing me with murderous eyes.

This was, of course, a clumsy attempt at face-saving. The implication was that he had thought I wanted to go to a sleepy and completely uninteresting little town—a place wrapped in peaceful slumber even in these stormy days—and that's why he had refused to let me in without a visa; had he known that I intended to go to Budapest where Russian tanks were being blown up and his own comrades strung up on trees, then he would have been only too pleased to oblige.

'I'm sorry,' I repeated. 'I failed to make myself clear. My fault.'

'I couldn't have guessed, could I?' he asked, his voice a shade less tremulous with homicidal fury.

'You should have let him in all the same,' remarked the leader somewhat ominously.

Five minutes later Crispian drove up. He was embraced and patted on the back by all the freedom fighters. I got into the car.

'Fancy meeting the author of *Horse Without Background* just like that. And the editor of—of . . . Well, to meet the editor, too,' said the little fat man.

'Thank you for your help,' I said to the leader which must have hurt the AVO man's pride.

'I didn't know you wanted to go to Budapest,' he repeated sulkily.

'Of course you didn't, Johnnie boy,' replied the leader of the revolutionaries, patting the AVO man affectionately on the back.

2

It is mostly Veronica that I remember from the Hungarian Revolution. Crispian and I quarrelled about her even before we met her. Crispian first mentioned Veronica on the second day of our stay. We were sitting in our hotel room (the staff were wonderful and service was almost normal) comparing notes. He said, unexpectedly: 'I'll go and see Veronica MacKay this afternoon.'

'Go, by all means.'

'You've heard, haven't you, that she's a ravishing beauty?'

'So I'm told.'

'Christ, I want to go to bed with her.'

I looked at him coldly. He added: 'She has quite a reputation, you know.'

His face bore a lewd expression. He looked like a lecherous schoolboy.

'You're a cad,' I told him.

'Why am I a cad?' he asked me, quite surprised. 'Don't you like going to bed with beautiful women?'

'Not with my friends' wives.'

'But Veronica isn't Sam's wife. They are divorced.'

'That's an excuse. He asked us to get her out of Hungary for him. As far as we are concerned, she's his wife. Or—to put it mildly—he seems to be still interested in her.'

'So am I,' he spluttered stubbornly, spitting in my eye as he was wont to do when excited. 'So am I, I tell you. They were divorced years ago. Didn't you hear that Sam cited nearly a hundred co-respondents?'

'It was only twenty-four.'

'Did you say "only"? I've heard people say it was a hundred. After that twenty-four sounds pretty small-time, almost virtuous.'

'It's all rumour, in any case,' I explained. 'In the end it was she who divorced Sam on grounds of adultery. And she has been living the life of a vestal virgin ever since.'

'The white flower of a blameless life, I'm sure. Nevertheless, there's no harm in trying.'

I am no puritan, but I still felt outraged. I eyed Crispian with contempt but he smirked back at me with a lecherous grin. I made a vow, then and there, that he wasn't going to have a chance of seeing Veronica alone. Two hours later on my way to Veronica—walking along the Boulevard—I was still fuming. Then I suddenly stopped and asked myself: 'Good God! I'm not jealous about Veronica Makkai, am I?'

I was in possession of her address—86 Coral Street, third floor, flat number 17—because almost every Hungarian newspaperman I met knew her, or at least of her. She lived in a two-roomed flat in a modern block behind the St Stephen Boulevard. There was a staggering shortage of accommodation in Budapest and I had heard (this I later found to be true) that she shared one of the tiny rooms with her aunt; the other equally diminutive room was occupied by a whole family: Mr Molnar—a clerk in a glue-factory—his wife and their fifteen-year-old son, Joseph.

Walking along the Boulevard to reach Coral Street, I had occasionally to duck into doorways when shooting flared up or moved too near, but it is amazing how quickly one grows used to the most abnormal conditions. Shooting, after a few days in Budapest, became something like rain: and as I did not have a bullet-proof umbrella, I had to shelter in doorways till it stopped. I had nearly reached number 86, when there was a deafening explosion. People grinned happily and nodded to each other. 'That was a Russian tank, blown to bits by a Molotov cocktail.'

I went up to the third floor of number 86 and rang the bell at flat 17. Veronica opened the door—there was no mistaking that wonderful red hair. I stood there with my mouth open, so taken aback was I by her expected yet unexpected beauty. She took my breath away. My heart beat faster—and I could not recall the simple appearance of a woman causing such a physical reaction in me for many, many years. She spoke to me before I could recover my breath.

'You must be Mr Matyas. I've been expecting you. Come in.'

I stepped inside and we stopped in the tiny hall.

'Expecting me? How did you know I was here?'

'In Budapest?' she smiled. 'Sam's best friend and envoy arrives here . . . how can I avoid hearing all about it in five minutes? Where is Crispian?'

I murmured some evasive reply.

'I want to talk to you, Matyas. We must have a chat. But I can't just now. I must take my Aunt Edith to the doctor.'

'What's wrong with her?'

'Nothing really . . . come and look at her.'

She opened the door of their room. At first glance I thought everything was wrong with Aunt Edith. In fact I thought she was dead. She was sitting in an armchair with her head thrown back, her mouth half open and staring icily into space. After a few seconds she started breathing heavily and moaning desperately.

'Veronica? . . . Is that you, Veronica . . . Jaj . . . Oooh . . . Ouch. . . .'

Veronica went into the room, put a small piece of ice into a kind of hose which looked like a misshapen hot-water bottle and put it—none too gently—on the old lady's forehead.

'Ouch . . . Jaj . . .' she moaned again miserably.

'She's a nuisance,' Veronica explained, coming back into the little hall, leaving the door ajar after her. 'She is terrified of the shooting. Terrified of death. I've never seen such a funk in all my life.'

There was a burst of firing a few streets away and Aunt Edith called out:

'Veronica . . . Come here, Veronica . . . You mustn't leave me alone. . . .'

'It's all right, Aunt Edith, it's only a bit of gunfire.' Then she went on talking to me: 'She says it's all due to the terrible experiences her late husband went through in the First World War.'

'You must be understanding,' said I.

'But as far as I can see her late husband had no terrible experiences in the First World War. He worked with the quartermaster general in a provincial town and in the spring of 1918 he ruptured himself. I don't think that quite justifies this panic nearly forty years later.'

A young woman opened the door of the other room.

'How is Aunt Edith?' she whispered, apparently much concerned.

'Thank you, Mrs Molnar,' replied Veronica. She sounded nettled by the woman's deep concern. 'I think she's fit as a fiddle. And fitter than my own fiddle. How am *I*, that's an entirely different question.' Then she asked, kindly: 'All is well with you?'

'I hope so. Both my husband and Joseph are out. I hope they'll return safe and sound.'

Mrs Molnar withdrew.

'Poor Veronica,' said I, using my sympathy to get on Christian-name terms with her.

'Well, I must take Aunt Edith to Dr Bild. It's just a few houses away. Come along with us if you like. The doctor is a friend of mine and he and his wife promised to look after Aunt Edith until this shooting dies down. The doctor said he would give her an injection whenever he—the doctor—needs a little peace and quiet. It *is* kind of them to take her in. They don't quite know yet what they're getting.'

It was not easy to persuade Aunt Edith to step out into the street, but luckily there was a lull and we reached the doctor's house without any incident or much fuss. We left Aunt Edith there in the care of the imperturbable Mrs Bild and, on our way back, I suggested to Veronica that we should go into an espresso. She agreed. We had a number of black coffees laced with several *baracks*—and talked about diverse subjects, including the problem of her coming to England. (Refugees were not leaving Hungary yet but the frontiers were wide open— as my presence there proved. She could have left whenever she wanted. Getting into Britain seemed a more formidable, if not an insurmountable, problem.)

'I don't know,' she said. 'Leaving one's country is not the easiest of decisions even at the best of times. I must think it over. To leave Hungary just now . . . I'm not sure I should approve of myself. We're winning, you know.'

She interrupted her musings and asked me: 'Does Sam really want me?'

'You must come,' I replied ambiguously and I was surprised to hear how hoarse my voice was.

'I'll think it over, Matyas. I need twenty-four hours for that. Not more—but one day I do need. Can we meet tomorrow?'

'Can we?' I thought. Yes, we can.

'I'll have to go to my work during the day, although there is some sort of general strike on and no one's really doing anything. But I'll try. Come to my place at nine in the evening.'

I promised I would.

'You'll have my reply: yes or no.'

'It must be yes,' I told her. This time my voice sounded cool and casual; as if I did not care.

3

Next day Budapest was buzzing with rumour; the Russians had apparently agreed to withdraw their troops from Hungary. People were hilariously happy as they awaited the official announcement which, indeed, eventually came. As the town was living in days of wild excitement and an atmosphere as far from normal as possible, it was regarded almost as a sacrilege to doubt that everything would turn out well. Whatever happened later, those were days of victory and delirious happiness.

I met Veronica at nine o'clock in the evening, as arranged. We went to the same espresso as before and had coffee and apricot brandy—the latter served in tiny liqueur glasses.

'I can't go with you to London,' Veronica informed me with a sad smile. 'It hasn't always been pleasant living in this country. Often it was hell. But it will be different now. You see, I hate big words as much as the next person. I haven't spoken or even thought of the "fatherland" since my schooldays.

But there are certain moral obligations one can't ignore. I'd love to be cynical, it's the fashion and I like being fashionable. But I can't, not just now, at any rate. You simply don't leave your country at such a time when the whole world— so it seems—is looking at us with a curious mixture of surprise and admiration. To leave now would be almost a betrayal.'

I took a deep breath and started on a long lecture.

'But you mustn't forget, Veronica, the other side of the picture. The revolution is, of course, not only a glorious but a very significant event and now that it has been clearly proved that a country *can* free itself from the Russians . . .'

She interrupted me with a smile.

'My answer is *no*, Matyas.'

I stopped.

'And that means no.'

That sounded a bit ominous.

It was about half past ten when we turned into Coral Street.

'Here's my key,' she said. 'Go up to my flat and wait for me. We'll have another drink. But first I must pay a short visit to Dr Bild to see how my dear Aunt Edith is.'

'Well, how is she?'

'Worse. Now that the shooting is dying down, she is more terrified than ever. She keeps telling me that all this reminds her of the terrible death of her husband on the battle-fields of the First War. But as poor Uncle Mark died of delirium tremens in 1936, it is not quite clear what she means.'

She was about to leave me when we heard a low call from a doorway:

'Veronica . . . Veronica. . . .'

It was Joseph Molnar, the young boy who, with his parents, occupied one of Veronica's two rooms. He looked dishevelled and the left arm of his jacket was badly torn. He rolled the tattered sleeve up and showed his arm.

'Can you do something with this?'

'Heavens!' exclaimed Veronica. 'You are wounded. What happened?'

'Nothing.'

'You must come with me to Dr Bild. This must be bandaged properly.'

'No, I can't. Honestly, I can't. I'm late, as it is. It's really nothing. Just a scratch. Just tie my handkerchief round this arm and it'll be all right.'

He produced one of the filthiest handkerchiefs I had ever seen in my life. Veronica examined the wound and pronounced it quite superficial. I gave her my handkerchief which happened to be spotlessly clean. She improvised a bandage.

'Don't breathe a word to my parents about this . . .' said Joseph. He spoke so fast that it was hard to follow him. First he talked in brief, staccato sentences, which—as he went on—grew longer and longer and more incoherent. 'They have no idea. They think I was playing football. In the park, with Paul Barany and other boys. But I wasn't, not really. Anyway, Paul Barany is dead.'

'What?' cried Veronica. 'That nice little boy?' (As if nice little boys never died.) 'But I saw him only yesterday.'

This wasn't a brilliantly intelligent remark but Joseph gave a worthy reply:

'Oh yes. But yesterday he was still alive.'

'What happened?' Veronica urged him. 'What on earth have you been up to?'

'Well, it was really Paul's idea. He said we should do something like the others and I said yes, we must but we didn't know what to do and how to begin. Then he heard that Captain Pakh, who used to be in the army, was organising boys in the basement of an elementary school near Rakoczi Street and we went there to see what's cooking. Well, we found Captain Pakh, but nobody asked who we were or what we wanted because there were a lot of chaps there and everyone kept going out and coming in again; it was all very confused and the Captain made a speech about the Soviet troops having been beaten by the revolutionaries and that now was the time to hit them even harder and things like that and then we all sang the National Anthem terribly out of tune. Then a few boys were given arms—most of them had guns already—and then the Captain said that once again he had to warn everbody that boys under sixteen were to go home because they mustn't fight. He told all boys under sixteen to step forward but no one did, not even a kid who couldn't have been more than twelve, I'm sure. There was a little more confusion about Paul and me because we belonged to nowhere but that was sorted out soon enough because a boy called Peter Halmi who was nearly nineteen said he could use us because three of his boys had been killed by the Russians the day before. That was a bit of luck. They gave us guns and we went off, about fourteen of us, to the Corvin Cinema and nothing really happened. Next day there was a lot of fighting with Russian tanks and we blew up two of them and it was great fun and none of us was hurt at all. The Russians ran off and someone started to sing the National Anthem but it did not catch on because you can't fight and sing at the same time, people only think you can but you can't really. And today there wasn't much fighting and we were happy because we had won and we were told that the Russians would soon be leaving and then suddenly the AVO started shooting from a third-floor window and they killed Paul Barany straight off and shot another boy in the leg and I got a scratch on the arm but it's nothing really and the main thing is that we have won and the Russians will clear out. The trouble was that I had to go to Paul's mother to tell her not to keep his supper for him and she started howling and crying and then she fainted and I didn't know what to do and it was awful.'

Veronica finished tying the bandage. She asked me to take the boy up and speak to his parents.

'You must not say a word to my parents,' Joseph protested

149

on the stairs. 'There will be a hell of a row if you do. My father does not approve at all of my fighting in revolutions. It would help if you could stay with me a little until the old boy calms down.'

But it was too late. Both his parents were standing on the staircase in front of the flat with the door wide open behind them. His mother's eyes were red and his father was furious. The boy stopped when he caught sight of them; so did I. There was deadly silence for a few moments.

'Come up,' said Mr Molnar in a dry, imperious voice.

Joseph went up and stopped, facing him.

'What sort of time is this to come home?' the father thundered.

Joseph gave no reply.

'How many times have you been told not to stay out after ten o'clock. Even that is late enough!'

Joseph remained silent.

'I suppose we have your dear friend Paul Barany to thank for this. I know his sort. I'll have a word with his father tomorrow.'

Still no word from Joseph.

'What have you been doing all the time? Don't try to tell me you've been playing football till this hour.'

Joseph did not try to tell him anything.

'And what have you done to your jacket?' bawled Mr Molnar. 'It's torn! Do you think I get my money for nothing?' He slapped Joseph's face. The blow rang throughout the building.

'But father . . .' Joseph stammered at last.

'Shut up!' his father roared and another slap followed. 'Go inside!'

They went in. I followed them.

I sat down in Veronica's room, waiting for her.

For about half an hour I could still hear the desperate sobbing of the little hero who had stayed out too late fighting in his revolution.

4

'It is a pity I can't go with you to London,' said Veronica pouring some sweet Hungarian liqueur into one of those tiny glasses. 'I should have loved to.'

She handed me a glass.

'Sam has married again, I hear.'

'Yes, he has.'

'Is his wife beautiful?'

'Quite pretty. But not what you'd call beautiful.'

'Is she well dressed?'

'No, she isn't.'

'Is it true that she is an artist?'

'Yes,' I replied a little hesitantly. 'You could call her an artist.'

Veronica sat down at the other end of the sofa.

'It's dangerous to live with artists.'

'It is very dangerous,' I agreed.

'Particularly for Sam, poor lamb.'

'Yes, particularly for Sam.'

'You sound very cryptic and mysterious.' Then, suddenly, she asked: 'Do you think he still loves me?'

I did not want to make a declaration of love in Sam's name.

'He asked me to take you to England,' I replied evasively.

'I behaved so absolutely abominably towards him that he must still love me. Artist wife or no artist wife.

'Damn this revolution,' she added after a little further reflection. 'Why did it have to start just now? And why is it so inspiring—such a fine thing? I should like to get out of here but now that I have a chance I cannot.'

'Don't mix things up, Veronica. If it hadn't been for the revolution, the Austrian frontier wouldn't be open and you couldn't get out in any case.'

'Yes, of course, it would be physically impossible. Now that it is physically possible, it has become morally impossible. Why must life be quite so complicated? I'd love to be liberated.'

I looked at her: 'You are a very beautiful woman,' I said softly.

'Perhaps I am. And perhaps that's the trouble with me.' She discussed my remark as if it had been a cool, impersonal, factual statement. 'Yes, I used to have reasonably good looks and the remnants of my so-called beauty are perhaps still discernible. It's no merit to be beautiful; but it has certain advantages. At least it has certain advantages while you are very young. Later? . . . Well, it's a mixed blessing. You are spoilt because of your good looks and spoilt children, as we all know, don't fare too well in life. I haven't fared too well myself.'

'May I ask you something, Veronica?'

'You may *ask*,' she smiled. 'The worst that can happen is that I shan't answer. But I most probably shall. The best way to wheedle out my secrets is to ask me straight questions. I always answer them.'

'Why did you do what you did to Sam? Was it to humiliate him? . . . Obviously if you live such a . . . well, I do not mean to be offensive, but if you are able to live such a virtuous life, you must have collected those twenty-four co-respondents out of sheer spite.'

'There were thirty-one co-respondents, really,' she said factually. 'There were only twenty-four on the list. In the heat of the moment I forgot seven of them.' Then her smile flared up. 'You seem to be very well-informed for a Londoner.'

'I knew nothing of all this in London. I met Andrassy in Belgrade.'

'You mean Jonathan Schwarz? . . . Has he been appointed riding master to Tito's children yet?'

'Tito has no children.'

'Bad luck for him. I mean for Jonathan. Not for Tito.'

'Indeed bad luck. He's head waiter in the Press Club.'

Veronica hardly ever smoked but she lit a cigarette now.

'I don't think it was out of spite.' She spoke thoughtfully. 'Of course, one never knows why one acts in the way one does. One always puts the most favourable interpretation on one's actions. We all want to cut a noble figure in our own eyes. I know all these motives, nevertheless I do think that I acted on an impulse of generosity.'

'Generosity?' I repeated the word with surprise.

'Yes: generosity. I wanted to *give*, you see. What more can you give than yourself?'

She spoke simply but seriously.

'You belonged to Sam,' I answered. 'You gave what was *his*. You were generous at his expense.'

'I'm sure I revolted against that notion, too. I wanted to prove that I belonged to myself and was nobody's chattel. They all wanted me so badly,' she went on. 'I felt inclined to be generous with them. My explanation may be utterly wrong; even silly.'

'Is that what you think now? That you were wrong? And silly? And that's why you live such a chaste life?'

'Oh no. Not because I've come to see the error of my ways. The spark of generosity has died in my heart, that's all.' She smiled. 'That's why I want to be liberated.'

I was sitting next to her by now. I turned her face towards me. She gave me a light kiss on my face and then she turned her mouth away. I put my hand under her skirt and rested it on her thigh—where the stocking ends and the flesh begins. She moved my hand away—gently but firmly.

'I'm Sam's wife,' she said.

'You are not. You were divorced ages ago.'

I remembered at that moment that Crispian had used the same phrase. I had thought it so despicable that I had nearly slapped his face. I still thought it was despicable but Veronica was maddening. Who was it who'd said: 'I can resist everything, except temptation'—and that was the best I could plead in my own defence.

'I shall probably never see Sam again. But in some way, somehow, I'm still his wife.'

I made another unsuccessful attempt to kiss her.

'I had pretty few scruples about me while I *was* his wife, I know. . . .' She looked at me with some hostility: 'He sent you for me. You are his best friend. Go away.'

I stood up and told her: 'You said you wanted to be liberated. Well, I don't want to liberate you.'

'Don't you?'

'No, I don't. I don't want to do you a "favour". I'm not going to give you back your generous impulses. I don't want to go to bed with you because it is good for your soul. I want it because it's good for my body. I want you because you are the most exciting and most desirable woman I've met for years. It's not Sam's friend that is talking to you now. It's the beast in me. Who wants the beast in you.'

She looked amused.

'You don't even pretend to love me?'

'No I don't. I am mad about you; but I don't love you.'

'You don't even hate me?'

'Good God, no. Hate is just another kind of love. I can't really explain. I don't love you; I don't hate you. But Heaven is my witness; I'm not indifferent to you.'

We were looking at each other now. I saw the fire in her eyes and I knew I had won.

'Let's go to bed, Veronica.'

She nodded.

'Let's.'

She slipped her clothes off and stood before me stark naked.

Later, she switched the light on and looked at me for a long time.

'You're a friend of Sam's?' she asked me seriously.

'I am,' I replied, slightly irritated because I did not want to discuss Sam just then and there.

'A good friend?' she asked.

'Yes. A good friend.'

She sat up and I could not keep my eyes off her breasts.

'You must be nice to him,' she added in a meditative tone, without a shade of irony or self-consciousness.

'Of course,' I nodded.

'Nice and loyal.'

'Nice and loyal,' I agreed and switched the light off.

FREEDOM FIGHTER

'Veronica,' said Sam when we got off the boat at Dover. Not 'Hallo, Veronica,' or 'How nice to see you, Veronica,' just the single word: 'Veronica'. Although he said it simply, without pathos, even without warmth or emphasis, I understood that he still loved her and would love her as long as he lived.

'Sammy,' said Veronica kindly. 'You've grown fat. It suits you. You look sweet.'

'This is my wife, Mariska,' said Sam, slightly embarrassed. Mariska looked spruce; she was turned out beautifully for the occasion.

'*Szervusz*,' said Veronica, extending her hand.

Szervusz, as I have already explained, is the greeting used between social equals of the upper and upper middle classes.

And now something pathetic happened. Instead of returning a casual and nonchalant *szervusz*, Mariska replied:

'*Kezét csókolom.*'

This is the Hungarian equivalent of the Viennese *Küss die Hand*—I kiss your hand—and, between women, it is the sign of one woman being the servant, or at any rate the social inferior, of the other.

There were two seconds of frozen silence. Perhaps it was one second only. But it seemed interminable while it lasted. Mariska—we all knew—had set out on this journey as a rebel; as a defender of her rights; defiant virtue, ready to face repentant sin. And it had all ended in surrender even before the battle was joined. If she had said: 'I know my place, Madam, I'm only a cook and I cannot possibly become the rival of a lady, like yourself,' she could not have made her sentiments clearer.

Veronica said: 'Oh, I've heard you're great fun, Mariska,' and she laughed gracefully as if this had been a capital joke. We all tried to laugh with her but it did not wash. Mariska knew as precisely as the rest of us that she had made a fatal mistake. Although later on she put up a spirited, indeed magnificent— if somewhat surprising—fight, she could never live down the impact of this first, single phrase.

'This is Aunt Edith,' said Veronica introducing her.

Sam's face fell—but only for a moment. Then his eyes lit up.

'How very nice to see you, Aunt Edith. Do you like country life?'

This question was a little unexpected. I thought, quite mistakenly, that Sam only wanted to make polite conversation and could think of no better opening gambit. However, Aunt Edith found nothing extraordinary in Sam's question and answered with a slight histrionic ring: 'Yes, I love peace and quiet. After all I've been through, a little peace and quiet is all I want.'

'You'll have it, Aunt Edith,' declared Sam firmly, glowing with satisfaction. 'I'm taking you to Bingerford-on-Taw.'

'Where is that?' asked Aunt Edith, terrified.

'In the West country, near Barnstaple,' explained Sam kindly. 'A region of great scenic beauty.'

A key to this mystery was soon supplied. Sam had been in utter despair on receiving my cable, sent from Vienna, informing him that Veronica refused to leave the country. The revolution seemed victorious and Veronica thought it was almost a crime to abscond—my message explained. Subsequently, however, events took a different turn. On the 4th of November the Russians came back with a vengeance. There was no point in staying now, and Veronica escaped with her aunt and 200,000 others to Austria. Veronica and Aunt Edith were among the first two or three thousand to leave and, for them, everything went smoothly. The loudspeaker at Budapest's Eastern Railway Station announced: 'Fast train to Szeged will leave at fourteen hours thirty-two from Platform 4. The Refugee Train to Győr will leave Platform 1 at fourteen hours forty seven.' The would-be refugees travelled to Győr, whence they proceeded by various means to border villages and from there again peasants—for a small consideration—led them across the frontier. Their mission successfully accomplished, the peasants returned for the next batch of refugees. Very soon all this changed. But for Veronica and her party the journey was so uneventful that—she told me later in Vienna—even Aunt Edith had no more than two crying fits and one single hysterical attack.

'London and England—in fact, as far as I can make out, the whole Western World—is crazy about Hungary and the Hungarian Revolution,' Sam told us. 'They are deeply impressed and, at the same time, deeply ashamed of themselves. They're ready to kiss the ground on which the Hungarians tread and, at the same time, they want to cover themselves with sackcloth and ashes. There has never been anything quite like this. And that is where Mr Hambleton comes in.'

'Who is Mr Hambleton?' I asked him, with growing uneasiness.

'John Hambleton. He's the mayor of Bingerford-on-Taw, in North Devon. Quite near Barnstaple.'

We looked at him because that failed to make it clear what Mr John Hambleton, the mayor of Bingerford-on-Taw, had to do with Aunt Edith.

'My life has been absolute hell for the last few days,' Sam explained when we settled down, a few minutes later, for what is called coffee in Dover. 'I just laugh with the purest *schadenfreude* at Matyas, who has no idea what is coming to him. Up to now some fifteen hundred Hungarians have arrived in London. The first thing they do is to ring me up.'

'All fifteen hundred?' asked Veronica.

'Oh no. It would be unfair to say *all*. Two failed to ring me up. Perhaps three. The rest did. They all say we were bosom friends in Budapest. Quite a few say that we are related. Yesterday nine first cousins of mine arrived. Even my elder brother has come to England although I am an only child. They are all journalists and they all want to write for *Bridge* or else want to sell their stories—with my help—to Hollywood film companies, at a minimum fee of £100,000.'

'Do they all have stories to sell?' asked Veronica. 'Lucky people.'

'They all have stories to sell. Every single person I have met was the real leader of the revolution. Everyone started it and fought it practically single-handed and everyone, without one single exception, was present at all major events. My elder brother excels even in such company: he was present at four different places at the same time. And that's not all: two of these events occurred outside Budapest.'

'You are a remarkable family, Sam,' said Veronica.

'But the Hungarians are not such a problem,' continued Sam, ignoring Veronica's remark. 'They are, as I've told you, only fifteen hundred as yet. (*As yet*, mind you: because if it goes on like this, the entire nation will soon be here. Apart from those who go to America.) Well, whatever the future may bring, fifteen hundred is a small figure. But there are more than fifty *million* Britons in this country. And they all ring me up, too. They're all crazy about Hungarians.'

'What do they want?' I asked.

'Various things. First of all, they want to help. There is a universal mania to help. They feel guilty for letting the Hungarian revolution down so they try to make up for this by sending blankets and warm underwear to the refugees. There are large centres where they can send donations or clothing and the addresses of these centres are given, every day, on the front pages of all newspapers and read out in all radio and television bulletins. But at least two hundred people ring me up every day and say, with that inimitable British courtesy, that they hate troubling me but as they are anxious to send some blankets and pants to refugees would I mind telling them where they can send them. The Trust for Christian Civilisation has engaged a secretary specially for this purpose: she tells them that it's no trouble, we are only too pleased to be of service, then she reads out the address from the front page of one of the popular dailies. They are overcome with gratitude; my special secretary reassures them that we are only too anxious to be of service.'

'But you still have not explained,' said Veronica, 'what Aunt Edith is to do in . . . where did you say?'

'Bingerford-on-Taw, near Barnstaple, North Devon. Well, Mr Hambleton, the mayor, came to see me this very morning. He was nearly in tears. He begged me to get a Hungarian refugee for him. A Hungarian hero. A freedom fighter. All the neighbouring villages have managed to get hold, by hook or by crook, of a Hungarian of some sort, but Bingerford-on-Taw is still Magyarless. He said his party would lose the next election if he returned to Bingerford-on-Taw without a freedom fighter.'

'But where are you going to get a freedom fighter for Mr Hambleton?' I asked Sam, suspecting the worst.

'I've got one already: Aunt Edith.'

Veronica dissolved in mirth.

'My dear Sam,' she said, 'you're quite mad. Madder than ever. I assure you Aunt Edith, far from being a freedom fighter . . .'

'Here you're wrong,' Sam interrupted her firmly. '*All* Hungarians are freedom fighters. By definition. Glorious sons and daughters of the revolution. And so is Aunt Edith.'

'Look,' said Veronica. 'Would it interest you to know that dear old Aunt Edith spent the revolution . . .'

Sam interrupted her again.

'It wouldn't interest me in the least. Nor would it interest the mayor or the people of Bingerford-on-Taw. She is a Hungarian refugee, *consequently* she is a freedom fighter and a heroine and that's that. To Bingerford-on-Taw you'll go, Auntie Edith, in the public interest. They have prepared a house for you—all furnished, even a bottle of milk is delivered at the front door and you can have that house free of charge for a year. Your larder is stuffed with the best tins Britain can produce and they've even got you a year's subscription to the *Tatler*. A magnificent civic reception has been prepared and no one is interested in the least—not in the least!—in what you were doing during the revolution. That's your private affair. And I must say one thing for the British, they never pry into people's private affairs.'

So Aunt Edith was sent to Bingerford-on-Taw the day after her arrival in Britain. A few days later Veronica was installed in a furnished flat near Earls Court—Sam got it for her for a year from a land-speculator who made millions by robbing poor people and who regarded the Hungarian Revolution as his private concern. Sam and Mariska returned to their flat in South Audley Street and—so it seemed—all settled down.

A fortnight later, having delivered my piece on Hungary to Crispian, I was off to Sydney, Australia, to collect materail for a sequel to my famous book, *Horse Without Background*, to be called *Kangaroo Without Background*. (Unfortunately, I'd had to shelve *Oh My Papa* for a while.) When I came back to London, after an absence of four months, I found a great many changes.

FORCE OF NATURE

I

I arrived back in my London flat on a Thursday evening—March 1957—at six o'clock. Half an hour later Mariska rang me up and asked me to come over to South Audley Street. I thought Sam wanted to talk to me urgently, so a few minutes after seven I rang their doorbell.

Mariska opened the door. I handed her the two books I had bought for her in Sydney. It was not easy to find Hungarian books for Mariska (she could read no other language) so I was delighted to pick up two novels in colourful paperback covers, one called *Damolino the Heartless Don Juan*, and the other *A Whip for Caesarina*, the latter being Number 613 in the *Sex and Crime* series. She accepted my gift with a tired smile, which was unusual because normally she was exuberant and volatile on receiving the smallest presents, let alone such magnificent ones.

'Do you want a drink?' she asked me with cool courtesy when I'd sat down in the large comfortable armchair.

'Good heavens,' I thought, 'she is picking up all the silly mannerisms of so-called society.' What would the world come to if even Mariska became just one of the many?

'Yes, Mariska,' I replied. 'I'd love a whisky.'

'Sweet or dry?'

'Medium,' I replied without hesitation.

The fact that she was obviously confusing whisky with sherry, somewhat reassured me. Mariska was not going to be lost in a colourless mass. I sighed with relief. I wondered how she would produce a medium whisky; in the end she handed me a drink which reminded me strongly of a dry Martini and it was quite drinkable.

I sat sipping my drink and said nothing. She sat down on the edge of a small chair, opposite me. She never felt quite at home in this new world of hers and always sat on the edges of chairs— never occupying more space than absolutely necessary. After a long pause she picked up *Damolino the Heartless Don Juan*, examined it carefully and declared: 'Looks good. Thank you.'

I nodded.

'A man must be terribly clever to be able to write a book like that,' she said with admiration. 'I wonder if it's all true.'

'I'm sure it is,' I assured her.

'You really think so?'

'I'm positive. I knew Damolino personally. He was a good friend of mine.'

She looked at me with admiration but soon reverted to her brand new melancholy smile. We sat there silently for another minute, then I asked her: 'Is Sam at home?'

She gave no reply.

'Isn't he at home? Where is he?'

Mariska snivelled and then burst out crying.

'Ask *her*,' she sobbed.

'Ask whom?'

'Her. Veronica. Ask her . . .' she said. 'He's gone . . . He lives with her.'

I cannot say that I was overwhelmed with surprise but I did find the situation most embarrassing. I searched my brain for some tactful and comforting words but could find none.

'I know I'm not the Eisenhover,' Mariska went on, 'but I am just as good-looking as that famous Veronica.'

I could not help feeling Mariska was taking the wrong line in this issue.

'I *am* sorry . . .' I muttered.

'I gave him everything he wanted. He put on four pounds in the last four weeks with me. A pound a week.'

'You are the most admirable cook I've ever met, Mariska,' I told her with warm and true conviction in my voice. This remark, however, turned out to be the worst possible thing to say.

'This has nothing to do with my cooking, Mr Matyas. Sam loved good food and I looked after him well. But he did not marry me for my cooking, after all. He married me because he loved me. It hurts me if you just praise my cooking.'

I looked at her in amazement. Not for a moment had it entered my mind that even Mariska could be in the slightest doubt as to why Sam had married her.

'If he had married me for my cooking,' she continued, 'he would never have left me. I can still cook better than Veronica.'

This last sentence was unchallengeable in its firm logic.

'I'm just as pretty as she is. I have better legs. I have nicer eyelashes.'

She did have, in fact, very nice legs although they looked a little too thin for her somewhat heavy body, and when I examined her eyelashes which I had never done before . . . well, I do not profess to be an expert on eyelashes. The last thing I look at in a woman is her eyelashes. But I took her word for that: she might have superior eyelashes. And yet, in spite of her eyelashes, I was surprised to find that Mariska was so determined to fight Veronica not on the ground of having nursed Sam better; not as a cook; not even as the lawful, wedded wife against the intruder and the thief—but as a beauty.

'I'm not an Eisenhover,' she repeated stubbornly, 'but I'm just as pretty.' (Presumably as Veronica, not as Eisenhower.) 'And I didn't go to bed with half Budapest . . . Not even with half Kis-Harsany.'

Then, after a short pause: 'Sam will come back to me. As long as he is happy with her, he'll stay away. But he'll come back when he feels unhappy.'

I made no reply.

'He gave me this flat but he says I ought to go back to America. But I will not go. I'll stay here. He is my husband and a wife should stay where her husband is—that's true, Mr Matyas, isn't it?'

'Every word of it.'

'I'll stay here because he'll come back to me.'

I said nothing.

'Do you think, Mr Matyas, that he'll come back?'

'No, Mariska. I don't think so.'

'You don't?' she asked me in despair.

'I don't. But I'm no prophet. He may, of course, but personally I don't think so.'

She sat there, pathetic and helpless. She picked up a small speck of dust from the carpet.

'I'm very busy,' she told me. 'We have five rooms and I must clean them every day. I've got no help now but I must keep it nice and tidy for him when he comes back. No one can say that the flat isn't clean. And I have to cook, too. It is not much fun doing all this cleaning and cooking just for myself, but what can I do? Well, that reminds me . . . Will you stay for supper?'

'What do you want to give me?'

'What would you like? I've got a chicken.'

'Paprika chicken then, with small dumplings.'

'And sour milk . . .' she nodded.

'Yes—I'll stay. Sour milk, of course.'

'But do you think he *may* come back?'

'Oh yes. He may,' I agreed.

'I know you think he won't. You've just said so. That's how I know. I've got a letter from Miss Markos. Martha. You know Miss Martha. She knows what's happened and she wrote to say that I could go back to her. She never filled my place, she writes. For old times' sake, she says.'

I expected her to follow this news with an angry outburst that she would not become anybody's maid and servant any more. But I was wrong again.

'Perhaps I shall go back,' she pondered. 'I'll wait a little. If you think Sam won't come back to me, I'll go back to them.'

I looked at her in amazement. The only matter of importance seemed to be that someone should go back to someone. Or was it simply, I wondered, that I—like everybody else—flattered myself that I knew something about human nature but I completely failed to understand even Mariska?

I met Sam and Veronica two days later. When I came back from Australia, they were enjoying a holiday in Torquay but they had to cut it short because Wilberforce S. Schmalz was coming over from New York and Sam had to meet him. Sam was not looking forward to this visit, not only because he disliked interrupting his holiday but because it was a sad and painful business: the sacking of Crispian Ransome-Hall.

'I shall have to drive out to the airport later on,' Sam told me on the phone, 'but not before eleven or so. Come and have a bite with us.'

Veronica and Sam were staying in Veronica's former flat near Earls Court.

'Poor girl,' Sam remarked when I told him that I had seen Mariska. Only the two of us were in the room, Veronica was busy in the kitchen.

'What do you mean by "poor girl"?' I asked him slightly irritated.

'Being left alone in London and all that.'

'Well, wasn't it you who left her alone?'

'What else could I do? I always liked her. I like her even better now. She's a wonderful old girl.'

'Don't be so damn patronising, Sam. You ruined her life.'

'But that's how it goes. We all ruin each other's lives, don't we? Veronica once upon a time, ruined mine; I ruined Mariska's; Wilberforce S. Schmalz is going to ruin Crispian's. That's life in general.'

'That means that you were fully entitled to ruin her life, if I understand you correctly,' I remarked.

'I couldn't help it, Matyas. I simply had to, you know. Force of nature.'

'You mean Veronica?'

He was annoyed: 'Of course I mean Veronica.'

'Mariska says you'll come back to her.'

Sam smiled at this but he went on talking about the other

subject: 'Besides, force of nature or no force of nature, I had to leave her if I wanted to stay alive. Dr Barna keeps a close check on me. He says I'm getting on all right. He's satisfied with my cardiograph. Only one thing can send me to my early grave, he says: overeating. But Mariska knew better; she had been told otherwise by that oracle of Kis-Harsany. And I couldn't resist her food. It's easy to say that I should have looked at her plum-dumplings but refused to touch them. You might as well have told Antony that it was all right to sleep with Cleopatra but he must not touch her. I had to leave Mariska; I had to run for my life. I had to come to Veronica.'

I did not need to ask Sam if he was happy or if he was in love. He would only have been embarrassed by a straightforward question like that and would have given some shy and evasive answer. It was enough to hear him utter Veronica's name; it was enough to see how he looked at her. They were a honeymoon couple. But 'force of nature'? Perhaps.

'She's wonderful,' he went on. He wouldn't have answered my question but he had guessed my thoughts. 'She's quite a bombshell, of course. Turns everyone's head. All the old fools are in love with her. And some of the young ones, as well. But she is used to that.'

I had some leg-pulling, jocular answer ready but suddenly thought the better of it and said nothing.

'In fact,' Sam went on, 'I'm a little annoyed with one particular person. Sir Henry Salami.'

This was the last name I expected to hear as the object of his jealousy.

'Enrico?'

'Oh, he's Sir Henry now. He got his knighthood in the Birthday Honours while you were in Australia. For his great services to literature and art. In other words for making it possible for Miss Sputz to win the Leo Doros Prize. People have been hanged for lesser crimes.'

'I must ring him up and congratulate him,' I murmured. So he scored a great victory over Percy Markham.'

'He did not, I'm afraid. Markham got a barony. He is Lord Ambleside now. For his great merits in getting people to drink his beer. And getting rich in the process.'

'You said Sir Henry . . .'

'It's nothing really,' he replied, obviously regretting that he had said anything at all. 'But he does annoy me by paying too much attention to Veronica. Courting her publicly in a jocular sort of way. I feel it is stretching a joke a bit too far. Well, let's drop the subject : here comes Veronica.'

After a few minutes she motioned us to the other end of the living-room which served as the dining-room. The table was beautifully laid, with the thinnest Rosenthal china, silver candlesticks, crystal wineglasses and napkins adorned with Brussels lace.

'You've got terribly anglicised, Veronica,' I told her.

She was badly bitten by the bug of anglomania, so this pleased her.

'Why do you say that?' she asked.

'Serving such bad food so exquisitely.'

She laughed.

'Well, Mariska is no Eisenhover; I'm no Mariska.'

'I do think, Veronica, your cooking is ideal to diet on,' I told her.

'A husband's best friend is even worse than the husband himself,' she replied laughing. 'You can't even throw things at him when he says things like that.'

What I said was no empty flattery; I meant it. We got grilled steaks—hard as leather—and Sam got nothing else. He was lucky. He was spared from watery, over-boiled potatoes with cold gravy, followed by warm ice cream.

'I'm on the wagon,' said Sam. 'I'm altogether a reformed character.'

'You're not exposed to very much temptation.'

'All right, Matyas, you've said enough,' Veronica grumbled.

Sam informed me that he was about to buy a house. They had already put down the deposit on a house in Hampstead, near the Heath, and it was a perfect beauty. They went on raving about it but I gained the strong impression that Sam hated the very idea of a house. Veronica must have talked him into it. She had set her heart on a house in England. To own a house in this country seemed to her the pinnacle of success and achievement.

'You're quite wrong, Veronica,' I tried to convince her. 'In England only those people become house-owners who cannot afford a flat. If a man can't pay rent, he borrows money and buys a house.'

'I want a house, Matyas. I want a house in England. It's true that we are rent-free here for a year; but Sam has to keep up the South Audley Street flat and maintain Mariska, so we really fall into the category which cannot afford a flat. Or another flat. We must buy a house. I assure you we are poor enough to buy a house.'

'You're doing a foolish thing. Take the word of an old friend who has lived here for donkey's years. A house is ideal for English people whose intellectual recreation is to paint the kitchen and redecorate the lavatory. And gardening, of course. I think it is their innate snobbery that is responsible for this mania for gardening. They all fancy themselves as landed gentry as soon as they produce a bunch of radishes and some peas. Leave houses to the English, Veronica. Stay in a flat. Houses are not for you. Besides, the house which you described to me is far too big for just the two of you.'

'But we won't be just the two of us,' she replied.

'Oh . . . congratulations. . . .'

'There's absolutely no reason for congratulations. Aunt Edith is coming to live with us.'

'Aunt Edith? . . . But I thought she was safely tucked away in Bingerford-on-Taw, living the happy life of the heroine of the Hungarian Revolution.'

'She is being hounded out of Bingerford,' Veronica explained. 'Public disgust with all things Hungarian coupled with her own personal unpopularity are getting too much for her. She can't take any more of it. Haven't you heard?'

As I had not heard a word, Veronica told me the story. Aunt Edith had been received like a Queen in Bingerford-on-Taw. There had been an official reception in the Town Hall, which was crammed with people, and a speech was delivered by Mr Hambleton of which she understood not one single word. But she had to give some sort of reply, so she replied in Hungarian. For weeks afterwards people made her life a misery with their kindness and solicitude. They brought her gifts. She received, among other things, twenty-seven teapots, a hundred and thirty-four embroidered tea cosies and three sets of golf clubs, and she was invited on the average to nine tea parties every week. Aunt Edith found these tea parties pretty dull affairs, even though she did not understand the conversation. No one really cared for her as a person: she was public property, the little town wore her, so to say, in its button-hole. Then, slowly, people wearied of, revolted, in fact, against their own guilt-complex. Who were these Hungarians, anyway? What did they owe them? What right did they have to expect or demand any-thing? So slowly they got fed up with Aunt Edith. They began to criticise her strange, foreign ways. They decided she was not showing herself grateful enough for the favours showered on her. Once she was observed talking rudely to a dog in the main street. (As she spoke to the dog in Hungarian, opinion was divided on this issue, some maintaining that Hungarian was simply a harsh-sounding language and that, in fact, she was impeccably polite to the dog.) There was, however, no doubt about the fact that she drank her tea without milk. She never even tried to play golf and she slept with her windows closed. She made disparaging remarks about English plumbing when her pipes froze for the fifth time in six weeks and this provoked the retort: 'Well, she shouldn't have come here if she doesn't like our plumbing.' Then someone in the village discovered that Hungary had actually fought on Germany's side in the war and—still worse—it became known that she regularly received a foreign type of sausage, known as frankfurters, from her niece in London and that she actually enjoyed eating them.

Bingerford-on-Taw started cutting Aunt Edith dead, no more invitations came her way, and in a few months it became abundantly clear that Bingerford and Aunt Edith had become mutually fed up with each other.

'But weren't there any other Hungarians in the district who could be helpful?' I asked Veronica.

'Yes, there were,' Sam replied for her, 'but they were even worse than the English. You see, they were of a different vintage.'

'I am speaking about Hungarian refugees, not Hungarian wine.'

'My dear Matyas,' Sam informed me with a knowledgeable air, 'your ignorance is sometimes shattering. The vintage year of a refugee is more important than the vintage year of wine. A man who immigrated here in the thirties, regards the post-war refugees as bloody foreigners and intruders into his country. He says things about them that even the most reactionary and xenophobe of Englishmen would not dream of uttering. Or take political refugees—resigned diplomats and other officials, for example. The right time to resign, each and every one of them will maintain, was the exact moment when he himself resigned. Anyone who fled abroad earlier than he did is a Horthy-ite, a Fascist, a reactionary beast who did not give the democratic régime a fair chance and was therefore himself responsible for the Communist take-over; anyone who resigned later is just a tool and lackey of the Communists. Believe me: it's all a matter of vintage.'

I protested that Aunt Edith had nothing in common with Iron Curtain ex-diplomats who had sought political asylum.

'But she's in the worst position of all,' replied Sam. 'The old refugees—the pre-war anti-Nazis and the post-war anti-Communists alike—who had a hell of a struggle to get residence permits and earn a livelihood, resent the fact that this post-revolutionary crowd is being offered visas and jobs—can decide, in fact, whether to condescend to choose Britain, America or Australia. *They* know perfectly well that Aunt Edith was no freedom fighter and, in any case, they maintain that the freedom fighters are ruffians and a bad lot. On the one hand they resent her for not being a glorious freedom fighter; but on the other hand they make it clear that they would resent her even more if she were one.'

The long and the short of it was that Aunt Edith was coming to live with them and poor Sam had to take the plunge. Buying that house meant serious obligations.

'I'll try to talk Wilberforce S. Schmalz into giving me a housing allowance. Even two thousand a year might help. But today they are not interested in anything except the orchestra.'

'What orchestra?' I asked.

'They are organising a Free Chinese—that is to say a Formosan Chinese—Philharmonic Orchestra to go on tour in South-East Asia. They are spending fortunes on that.'

'Sounds a brilliant idea.'

'It is. Because what are the needy people of Laos and Cambodia clamouring for? For a Free Chinese Philharmonic Orchestra to play Haydn and Mozart to them but not—I'm sure—Shostakovitch or Borodin.'

The time came for Sam to go to the airport. We'd had so much to talk about that it was only now he told me about Crispian's plight. The New York office of the T.C.C. had gone crazy, he complained bitterly. They were determined to sack Crispian Ransome-Hall.

'But why on earth?' I asked.

'Mostly because firing people is an American mania. They have to fire people to boost their ego. Firing gives them a sense of power. The excuse this time is that Crispian is too anti-Communist and anti-Russian.'

'But that's what the T.C.C. was founded for, wasn't it? To fight Communism.'

'No. They say I spoke of a bridge on that first night and that even our periodicals are called *Bridge*. We are aiming at *rapprochement* not cold war. I've tried to explain that all this was sensible before the Hungarian Revolution but is quite out of date now. Communism has shown its ugly face and we must fight it. But Wilberforce S. Schmalz says that the Council hold different views. They want a bridge; they want *rapprochement*.'

'Poor Crispian,' said Veronica.

Sam nodded gravely. He had written to Schmalz ten days before, explaining that Crispian was a true bridge-man. One of his poems from *Lightbrown Thursdays* had been republished in *Peace and People*—a real fellow-traveller organ if ever there was one.

'That seemed to have satisfied them,' Sam continued. 'I thought the matter was closed. But it isn't closed at all. Far from it. That's the main reason for Schmalz's visit here. To hell with Schmalz!' he said and left for the airport.

'What is this gossip I hear about Sir Henry Salami?' I asked Veronica when we settled down for a drink.

'Oh, the old boy fell for me a little bit, that's all. Nothing serious. He wants to take me to Barbados on a little holiday. A pleasure cruise, we might call it.'

'And what has Lady Salami to say to this? Does she agree?'

'She's a well-trained Italian signora. She would pretend to know nothing.'

'But I do hope, Veronica . . .' I began solemnly.

'Stop it, Matyas. You needn't say a word. Of course the whole thing is utter nonsense.'

'Glad to hear it. You mustn't look at the old fool.'

'Thanks. You, as a loyal friend, want to convince me that I must remain faithful to Sam. And if, for some unfathomable reason, I don't, then I should go to bed with you and no one else. Is that it?'

'Veronica, my love, you express yourself with greater clarity than I like in such cases. Nevertheless, that was the gist of what I meant to say.'

She shook her lovely red head.

'Nothing doing, Matyas. I love Sam. I'm grateful to Sam. I don't want Sir Henry Salami. I don't want you. I don't want anybody else, only Sam. I'll be a model wife because he's a model husband. I've arrived in a haven: I want Sam, our new house and nothing, absolutely nothing, else.'

'Except Aunt Edith perhaps,' I remarked, just to be nasty.

'It's no good, Matyas. Nothing doing.'

Well, that's that, I said to myself walking home in the night. Certainly quite a lot had happened while I was away in Sydney. Sam had left Mariska; Aunt Edith had left Bingerford-on-Taw; Crispian was going to leave the T.C.C.; Veronica, in a sense, had left me. People, alas, were settling down at last, I thought, with great regret. 'A pity,' I reflected and thought of Veronica. If, from now on, I was loyal to my friend, it wouldn't be my fault.

But my fears—even if things turned out differently from what I anticipated—were premature. There is never any danger of adults growing up.

SCHMALZ'S VISIT

I have no personal knowledge of what happened between Sam and Wilberforce S. Schmalz, but Sam subsequently told me about their conversation.

Wilberforce S. Schmalz missed his plane in New York and arrived only the following day at 3.45 p.m. Sam drove out to the airport for a second time, picked him up and was driving him to the Savoy. Wilberforce S. Schmalz, in addition to being an eminent attorney, was also a man of action and always came to the point without beating about the bush. This time, too, he started discussing his errand with Sam as soon as the car had left London Airport.

'I've got two things to tell you, Sammy boy.'

This 'Sammy boy' struck Sam as ominous. Schmalz had never called him 'Sammy boy' and Sam, as far as he could recollect, had never offered sufficient provocation to be addressed in this way. Wilberforce S. Schmalz seemed embarrassed. Some men when embarrassed, blush; others call people 'Sammy boy'.

'I've got two things to tell you, Sammy boy. One good, one bad.'

'Out with it. Tell me the bad one first.'

'I've got to tell you the good one first. I am glad—real glad—to be able to tell you that your viewpoint prevailed with the Executive Council of the T.C.C.'

'What viewpoint?' asked Sam suspiciously.

'About co-operation with the Russians. That bridge or no-bridge business. You remember, you suggested that now we ought to take a tough line.'

'Well, I'm all for co-operation and co-existence and all that. Only in view of what has happened in Hungary . . .'

'Sure. Sure thing, Sammy boy. That's what I have in mind. The Council, at its last meeting but one, was all for co-operation and for closer ties with the Reds. We wanted to be real good friends with those damned Reds.'

'Quite,' Sam nodded.

'There was one voice only which said: "We must get tough with them, after what they've done in Hungary!" That voice was yours. And your voice prevailed in the Executive. It's true that John Foster Dulles started saying the same thing. Admittedly, that may have had something to do with their decision, too. We are a completely independent body, mind you. But we are entitled to listen to what the Secretary of State has to say. Co-operation and co-existence are dead. We're going to take a real tough line. Believe me, boy, that's quite a triumph for you. Heartiest congratulations.'

'Thank you,' said Sam coolly. 'Even if I have to share the honours with John Foster Dulles. . . .'

There was a brief silence.

'That means,' said Sam at last, 'that Crispian's job is safe.'

'Not quite,' Wilberforce S. Schmalz shook his head. 'No, it doesn't mean that.'

'But surely,' Sam argued excitedly, 'if he was dismissed *because* he took a tough line vis-à-vis the Communists and now this tough line has become our official policy, that means that he's been fully vindicated.'

'Sure it does mean that,' Wilberforce S. Schmalz agreed. 'Sure thing. But you yourself drew our attention to his poems— *Lightbrown Something or Other*—appearing in *Peace and People*. And we found out that another one, *Tophats and Canaries* had appeared there some time ago. You do see, Sam, don't you that we can't have editors who have their lightbrown whateveritis published in Red magazines.'

'Lightbrown clashes with red . . .' Sam remarked with bitterness.

'Everything clashes with red,' Wilberforce S. Schmalz laughed heartily. He was pleased with this *bon mot* and repeated ft three times, as if he and not Sam had said it in the first place.

By now Sam was so worried that he nearly ran into the lorry immediately in front of him. He felt angry and indignant but was careful enough not to be carried away by these sentiments. That he himself should be responsible for Crispian's downfall; and that Crispian's neck should be broken by the very weapon he had brought up in his defence, was a thought hard to bear.

'But that was one single isolated occurrence, Wilberforce,' he began with great self-discipline. 'It came about in quite exceptional circumstances . . .'

'If I were you, Sammy boy,' Wilberforce S. Schmalz interrupted him, lighting a cigar and puffing heavily, 'I shouldn't be bothered too much about that Ransome-Hall guy.'

'But he's a friend of mine, Wilberforce. One of my close friends. And don't you see that I feel responsible for his fate though I was really trying to help him when I informed the Council through you that . . .'

'I shouldn't be bothered all the same. Because—and that's the bad thing I've got to tell you—they are terminating your contract, too.'

'Mine?' said Sam, firmly convinced that he had misheard.

'I don't like telling you this, Sammy boy. I'm not enjoying it at all. Sure I'm not. But you do see our point, don't you?'

'No. I don't see it. What *is* your point?'

'Goodness me, after all you are the father of this bridge idea. Of co-operation. And Red-loving.'

Sam did not feel like arguing.

'So I'm fired?'

'No, no, you are not fired. Your contract is terminated.' And as an afterthought: 'You are only sort of fired to that extent.'

'But only to that extent?'

'Sure thing. Your contract is terminated. That's all.'

'Oh, is that all?' asked Sam rejoicing.

'Sure thing. That's all.'

'Besides,' Wiberforce S. Schmalz went on, 'Hungary is

rapidly becoming less and less important. It's all the Afro-Asians now. You must have heard of our Free Chinese Philharmonic Orchestra. It's a great achievement. It was the idea of Mrs Leo Doros. Lucky guys those Afro-Asians, I can tell you that. We are organising a conference at Ogbomoshu, I think in Nigeria or thereabouts, and guess what's going to be the main subject for discussion. "The Responsibility of the Intellectuals and the Creative Imagination." No more difference, sonny boy, between white people and coloured people. Those times are over. Which is real lucky for those damn niggers. . . .' And after a long puff at his cigar: 'They may even get a Leo Doros Prize, the bastards. . . .'

But Sam had stopped listening.

When they arrived at the Savoy, Wilberforce S. Schmalz reassured Sam that he could come to him to discuss any problem at any time and he would be only too glad to help him in any way he could.

'But you can't do anything about my job?'

'Not a thing. Not about that. But if you have any other problem just come to me. I'm your real good friend, Sammy boy.'

Sam did have a problem and he was back at the hotel in two hours. Could he go over to New York, he asked, to discuss matters with members of the Executive? Wilberforce S. Schmalz was not enthusiastic about that suggestion—he had spoken after all—but, after about half-an-hour's wrangling, he gave in. In a manner of speaking Sam was the founding father of the Trust of Christian Civilisation and had influential friends. He had the ear of Borsch, P. T. Trotter, Earl F. Millington and other important guys and Schmalz was worried lest it be held against him if he refused Sam's request.

'We'll have your first class jet ticket ready whenever you want it.'

'Tourist class will do,' Sam replied with a melancholy smile.

'Out of the question,' shouted Wilberforce S. Schmalz with indignation. 'Tourist class for *you*?' Out of the question. . . .'

Sam went home and sank into an armchair. He could not tell Veronica what had happened. His dismissal meant that the idea of the house had to be given up. And it meant a great deal more—the onset of financial worries, joblessness, a drab and insecure existence. He knew this only too well. No, he could not face Veronica. She realised, of course, that something was wrong but never suspected the magnitude of the calamity. She probed a little, asking questions—gentle, friendly, even facetious questions—but when Sam acted as though he did not hear her, she shrugged her shoulders and went off to open some tins for dinner.

Sam suddenly jumped to his feet, walked out of the flat, slamming the door behind him, and began to roam the streets of London as he had roamed, in another crisis of his life, the streets of Budapest. He left Earls Court and walked on and on, without paying any attention to where he was going. A world had collapsed, it became clear to him, an era of his life was coming to an end, at the worst possible moment. He was going to lose Veronica again, he thought, and despair smote him. He felt his forehead: It was ice-cold with sweat. In misery he leaned against the wall of a house. He looked round. He was in South Audley Street. He lifted up his eyes to his own windows—they were all dark.

There he remained standing for ten minutes. For an hour. Or perhaps two hours. He had no idea.

But Mariska had noticed him soon after his arrival. She ran to the kitchen and started cooking, making periodic trips back to the window to keep an eye on the dark, shadowy figure at the corner.

At last she opened the window and called out: 'Sam!'

He did not seem to hear her.

'Sam!' she called for the second time.

He looked up.

'Dinner is ready, Sam.'

He shook his head.

'I can't . . . No, I can't, Mariska. . . .'

'It's plum-dumplings, Sam.'

He shook his head, even more firmly.

'There's goulash to go with it.'

'No . . .' he said hoarsely. 'I don't want . . .'

But he started moving towards the house like a sleepwalker.

'Thank you, Mariska . . . But I can't . . .'

'Goulash to start with, plum-dumplings to follow,' she repeated and shut the window.

And he followed the alluring voice and had no idea why; no more idea, anyway, than the cobra has why *it* follows the alluring flute of the snake-charmer.

TWO WIVES' TALES

'Yes, I noticed him all right, Mr Matyas,' Mariska told me when Sam was already in the air, flying towards New York. 'I looked out of the window a lot because I was always expecting him. There he was, leaning against the wall of the house opposite—well, not quite opposite, that one over there, you can see it if you look out from here—and he was looking miserable and hungry. I don't think he was properly fed, Mr Matyas, if you ask me.

'So I went and prepared a meal for him. I made goulash and plum-dumplings because he liked those, and you may remember that one day, in Nave-York when we were still at Miss Martha's place, he ate the same dinner with a healthy appetite.'

'Oh yes, I remember,' I assured Mariska. 'There was no reason then for worrying because of his appetite.'

'Plum-dumplings are good for him. They build up his strength. And that's what he needs. If you are ill you've got to be well fed—built-up-like—whatever these newfangled doctors try to tell you. I remembered, his great ambition was to eat fifty of them, almost twice as much as your cousin Laci could in Transylvania, when you were little boys. That was his great ambition, Mr Matyas, and I did not blame him for it. We all have our ambitions.'

That was the first axiomatic statement I ever heard from Mariska. But not the last.

'You know, Mr Matyas, I've been thinking over what we were talking about that last time you had dinner with me. Paprika chicken with sour cream and small dumplings. Remember?'

Yes, I did remember.

'I wanted Sam to come back to *me*, not to my cooking, if you know what I mean. You have read so many books, Mr Matyas, and you find the same things in so many films, too. Millionaires and rich people always want the girl to love them for their own sake and not for their money, if you see what they mean.'

'I don't quite see what they mean, Mariska. I never could see it. My own ambition in life—and as you've just said, we all have our ambitions—is that a number of beautiful, eighteen-year-old girls should love me madly for my money.'

'I'm not sure I've got you, Mr Matyas, but I didn't mind any more if Sam was coming back to me for my cooking. A woman who can cook well, after all, is a good wife to a man who loves to eat well.'

'And a masochist, then, surely must be an excellent wife for a sadist,' I thought sarcastically but I felt immediately ashamed of this thought. Of course, a masochist *is* a good wife for a sadist. We all seek different partners in life. These short months of loneliness, I pondered, had done a great deal of good to Mariska's reasoning abilities.

'If *I* can cook well, Mr Matyas, then the cooking is also *me*, if you know what I mean. I used to be angry with Sam when he said that no one could make plum-dumplings like me. But he meant it kindly, really. The plum-dumplings I make are also me, Mr Matyas, if you follow me. I knew a woman, back in Nave-York, a friend of Miss Martha's who wanted to become a painter and paint so beautifully that men would admire her for paintings but when they did she got angry because she wanted to be loved for herself. I couldn't paint for Sam, Mr Matyas, or dance for him or whatnot. But I could cook, and when you left after that paprika chicken with sour cream I thought and thought about it and I began to see that those plum-dumplings are also me. Part of me, Mr Matyas, and they become part of Sam and they make for a certain unity between us, if you know what I mean.

'So I called to him to come up from the street and he shook his head and said he couldn't come but he came all right and I know now that he wouldn't have come for my sake alone and he wouldn't have come for the dumplings alone either: he came for both of us. Or perhaps it is wrong to say, "both of us" because he knew that me and my dumplings, we're really one.

'When he came in the goulash was already on the table and it was piping hot, too. And we talked as we ate just as we used to, and he teased me, he always liked teasing me but I didn't mind. I said nothing to him about having left me and he said nothing about it, either. He told me the goulash was out of this world and that I was a grand girl and I must not be cross with him if he didn't eat too much because he wasn't supposed to. Then I brought in the plum-dumplings and smiled happily and the dumplings smiled back. I am speaking the truth, Mr Matyas, I saw them smile back. Then he said: "To hell with everything, Mariska, today I'll reach the fifty", and I said: "You can do it, Sam, I know you can do it." Because a man needs some encouragement from a woman, Mr Matyas.

'While he was eating his dumplings, I went to our bedroom and changed because I had no time to change before and I wanted to look nice and . . . well, I wanted to look really nice, if you know what I mean. And then . . . then . . . I don't know why I'm telling you all this, I'm sure I shouldn't, but I took the cover off the bed because . . . well, I just did.

'I went back to Sam who had had twenty-two dumplings by then. He was quite happy and said a lot of silly things. He was a little drunk, food always makes him a little drunk—I don't know how this works but it does. He said we were colleagues, the two of us, because cooking and producing a magazine were the same thing. When I said, "Don't be silly Sam", he said, "Why, you work for hours and hours on a dinner and then I come and gobble it up in a few minutes; and I work for weeks and weeks on the magazine and my silly readers finish it in an hour or so!" And then I told him again not to be silly but he shook his head sadly and said that he wasn't even an editor, he was only a kind of charity-man, except that my cooking was doing more good to humanity than the Trust of Christian Civilisation which is a silly thing to say, as my cooking isn't really Christian, if you follow me. He ate more and more plum-dumplings and started breathing heavily and said that we both were finished—we were colleagues in that, too—I had no one to cook for and he had no one to be charitable to. When he got to his fortieth dumpling he was talking more and more hesitantly . . . sort of tipsy, Mr Matyas . . . and he said he shouldn't eat all these dumplings because they'd kill him but he laughed a sort of drunken laugh and said that he'd rather be dead and happy than alive and miserable. That wasn't a very Christian thing to say, either. And he went up to forty-five and I said, "I'm sure you can make the fifty, Sam" and he said, "No, Mariska, I can never achieve what I want. Never. Not quite, anyway"—and you know, Mr Matyas, he was dead right because he reached forty-eight and then swallowed one more with great difficulty, moaning and gasping for air . . . that made it forty-nine . . . and then he passed out. He stood up and embraced me and kissed me on the cheek and I helped him to the bedroom. He leaned on me and I supported him and he said: "I love her . . . I love her . . ." He didn't say who he meant but I knew only too well. And when he got to the bedroom he fell on the bed and slept—in his clothes, as he was—for the whole night and the next day and the whole night after that, which makes it two nights and a day between, Mr Matyas.'

'And that was all?'

'That was all. He got up on Thursday morning and said he had a terrible headache and felt miserable but I'm sure he thought it was Wednesday. I offered him breakfast but he shook his head. He kissed me on the cheek again and said I was wonderful and a real friend and he left in a hurry.'

That was the end of her story and she fell silent. Then she blushed and looked at me. She hesitated for a moment before she spoke again: 'No, he didn't sleep with me. I can't say he did. But he slept with my plum-dumplings.'

'And do you know, Matyas, where he was for two nights?' asked Veronica, her eyes flashing with anger. 'With Mariska. Two nights and a whole day.'

'But you don't know what he was doing there.'

'I can guess.'

'No, you can't, Veronica . . .' I started but did not get far.

'Don't try to tell me that he was eating plum-dumplings and that was all, Matyas. Not even Sam could eat for two whole nights. He didn't say one single word to me before he left. As if I had been guilty of something. I, who loved him; I, who lived the life of a saint. He just packed his suitcase and left for New York. I could see he wanted to speak to me, but he didn't. Do you know why he behaved like that, Matyas?'

'Yes, I think I do.'

'So do I. Because he wanted to pay me back for all the suffering I had caused him. He wanted to pay me back in kind. I thought he had forgiven me. I even thought he'd never hated me for it. I thought he still loved me. What a fool I was! He only wanted his revenge. He had it all planned for ages. He wanted to humiliate me, to spit on me. And I, poor fool, was loyal and faithful to him.'

'Now don't be idiotic, Veronica. . . . You know Sam better than to believe that.'

'I am talking sense, Matyas, and you know it. To plan a revenge for so long . . . and so meanly . . . it's inhuman.'

'Veronica . . .'

'It's inhuman, Matyas. It's beastly. He didn't go back to Mariska because he loved her; not because he found her irresistible. Just to humiliate me. And why did he stay away two nights without a word, a message—some stupid excuse? Because he wanted to lay it on thick.'

'You've got to listen to me, Veronica. I'm going to tell you the whole story.'

'There is no whole story. I'm not going to listen to anyone.

I'm going to tell *you* something, Matyas. No one can do *that* to me, Matyas, and get away with it. Little Sam is not going to make a fool of *me*. If he thinks he can laugh at me, we'll see who'll have the last laugh. . . .'

She went to a small bureau—this conversation was taking place in her flat—and waved a small green book at me.

'My travel documents, Matyas. That's why I asked you to come up. Please to tell your friend, Sam MacKay—whenever you see him—that I've gone off to Barbados with Sir Henry Salami. Give him my kind regards. And goodbye to you, too. That's all I wanted to say.'

BARABBAS

Two days after Sam's departure Wilberforce S. Schmalz asked me to go and see him at the Savoy. He was feeling uncomfortable about Sam and wanted me to fly over to New York to help him and—as he put it—to see what was cooking. He wasn't a bad guy, Wilberforce S. Schmalz, and he liked to squander T.C.C. money as much as the next man.

I accepted his offer with avidity. First of all, I was keen on helping Sam although it was not quite clear what I could do. Then I'd had a message from Allyears, who had read my detailed synopsis of *Kangaroo Without Background* and said they wanted to see me urgently. (It turned out eventually that they only desired to inform me through my editor, Miss Eleanor Sputz, that they still did not like my writing and that *Kangaroo Without Background* had only confirmed the low opinion they had hitherto had of it.)

'I'm going to do something I've never done in my life,' said Sam when we were sitting together once again in the lounge, or to be precise, in the lobby, of the Potomac Hotel. 'I'm going to beg them to save me. I'll implore them. I'll bully them. I'll make a nuisance of myself. I must keep that job.'

I scratched my head.

'I've already spoken with most of them. They are quite sympathetic, the bastards.'

I offered him my help. Here at last I could do something practical. He'd already had a word with Borsch but I promised to see him again to make sure of his support. I told him that I would have a word with Mrs Doros, too, and remind her that it was we two, between us, who had made her late lamented husband pretty immortal. Sam had already seen P. T. Trotter, too, and was to have a chat with Earl F. Millington that afternoon.

'I talked to him on the phone yesterday,' Sam informed me. 'He's going to Europe in two or three days. I hope he's not going before the next Executive Meeting. That would be a blow. I'm sure I can count on the old boy—and d'you know why?'

'Why?'

'Because he regards Mariska as one of the greatest wits he's ever met. Well, when I think of the wits he is likely to meet . . . Anyway, he'll do what he can for her sake.'

'Don't you think that's a bit immoral?'

'What is?'

'To use Mariska's influence—whom you left—to save your job for Veronica?'

He looked at me in surprise.

'You *are* squeamish, aren't you?'

He added with a broad smile: 'By the way, do you know what Earl F. Millington wants me to do? He is sailing to Southampton in the *Egalité* and he suggested I should go with him. Wouldn't you like to go instead? Five days of intense communion with Earl F. Millington would be an exhilarating experience.'

'No, I must fly home, Sam. Thanks all the same. What did you tell him?'

'I told him it was a fascinating idea and although it was awfully difficult to spend five days travelling instead of five hours or so, I'd do my best because I'm simply longing for his company.'

2

The Executive met in two days' time and turned Sam's request down unanimously.

'The swine,' I said to Hazay-Hirschfeld, whose guest I was for a drink in the Waldorf-Astoria. We were waiting for Sam who was late.

'Swine? Why?' he asked.

'They all promised their support. Well, not all—we couldn't speak to all of them. But four or five determined friends should have been able to sway the Executive. But, as you've heard, the decision against him was unanimous. They all let him down.'

'Did you say "swine"?' he asked again, pondering over the expression and weighing it up.

'I did.'

'Well, swine they certainly are. But for different reasons.'

'Not for letting Sam down?'

'They didn't let Sam down,' he declared firmly.

'How can you say such a thing?'

'You have no idea how these things are dealt with at Committee meetings. Have you ever read that wonderful story of Karinthy's, *Christ or Barabbas*? The crowd outside Pilate's palace is given the choice of saying who is to be spared and set free: Christ, God's son, or Barabbas, the thief? All the people there, as *individuals* shout "Christ!" but the answer of the *crowd* is: "Barabbas!" A few hundred individuals shout "Christ!" yet their answer becomes "Barabbas!" That's all.'

'Yes or no for Sam, you mean?'

'Quite,' Professor Hazay-Hirschfeld nodded gravely. 'When the question was put whether Sam should be saved, all the *individuals* present shouted an enthusiastic "Yes!" Yet, the answer of that mob called the Executive was a resounding "No". So Sam will be crucified. It's always the thieves who are saved. Our friends and their colleagues on the Executive would crucify their own mothers if (*a*) social prestige required it, and/or (*b*) it meant a really good profit. Let's be fair. I said "really good profit". They wouldn't crucify their mothers for a paltry sum. Nothing under a thousand bucks, tax paid.'

'That means, of course,' I said after a while, 'that Crispian Ransome-Hall is sacked, too.'

'Don't you worry about Ransome-Hall,' retorted the Professor and ordered the fourth round of dry Martinis. 'He's got a job. I fixed him up.'

'You?' I asked.

'Yes, me. You know my racket. Don't say you don't. Everybody does. I tried to keep it secret for a long time but it has been generally accepted, practically sanctioned by now, so why this cloak of secrecy? Surely, I'm a more honest crook than the rest of them; and better educated. Besides, it is Big Business now, and Big Business is always respectable, however dirty it may be.'

'You were telling me about Crispian Ransome-Hall.'

'Oh yes. It's all very simple. You know we were sending these books to Hungary—to Szeged—and they were sent back. Ransome-Hall invented a method by which *we do not have to send the books at all*. It's marvellous. All we have to do is take the money. It saves us a lot of trouble; and a lot of unnecessary expense. We can cut down on staff, too. So Ransome-Hall is going to get part of our savings. At the present rate that means about five or six thousand dollars per annum. Not a fortune, but he can live on it. We've all lived on less, at one time or another. In any case, he wants to give most of his time to writing poetry. He is already working on the continuation of *Lightbrown Thursdays*.'

'*Lightbrown Fridays*, I suppose.'

The Professor shook his head.

'*Lightbrown Wednesdays*. Don't forget: he's a progressive poet.'

'How is Miss Sputz?' I asked.

'Don't ask me,' he replied grimly. 'She left me. She managed to find a poorer man.'

'But younger, I presume.'

'He's eighty-four. Eleanor always preferred a mature type.'

Sam arrived and to my delight he was in the best of spirits.

'Damn them all,' he said with a grin. 'I managed to live somehow, before the Trust for Christian Civilisation was dreamt up.'

'Don't kid yourself,' said the Professor. 'A former Foundation man stinks. He is generally hated and despised. It doesn't matter that this is a racket. The trouble is that it's a good racket.

Too many people try to jump on the wagon; and those who don't succeed hate the luckier racketeers.'

'Well, perhaps to some extent . . .' Sam tried to continue but the Professor went on with his discourse.

'And alas, or fortunately—I cannot decide which—the Foundations do appoint nincompoops to high places who, but for the Foundation, would be rotting as third-rate toilers somewhere on the peripheries of literature. It won't be easy, MacKay. Should you, however, wish to become a criminal and join my organisation . . .'

This time Sam interrupted him:

'We'll have to tighten our belts for some time, that's all. Veronica will understand, I'm sure. She can work. And if the worst comes to the worst, I can work, too.'

He seemed quite happy or, at least, he was accepting the situation with a stiff upper lip and a stout heart. The suspense was over and he looked relieved. We chatted for a long time, telling each other T.C.C. stories. Sam periodically returned to the subject of his future plans—he was bubbling with ideas. He even had two dry Martinis, a rare occurrence for him as he hardly ever touched alcohol. An hour later he was in buoyant mood.

We decided not to break up but go out and have dinner, the three of us.

'You're my guests,' said Professor Hazay-Hirschfeld. 'I'll take you to the Ocean Wizard. The food is bad but sufficiently expensive.'

'Invitation accepted,' replied Sam. 'But if we're going out I must go up to my room and wash and perhaps change.'

The T.C.C. had put him up in the Waldorf-Astoria. They had offered to put me up there too and were a little disappointed when I decided to stick to the Potomac.

When Sam came back a quarter of an hour later, he was holding a picture post-card. He thrust it into my hand, without uttering a word. I looked at the picture first. It showed a pleasant view of Barbados, with a charming bay and a number

of small boats, with red, blue, green and yellow sails. I turned it
over. It read:

> *I'm having almost as pleasant a time here
> with Sir H. S. as you had with Mariska.*
>
> *V.*

'Do you know anything about this?'

'Yes. I do.'

'So it's true?'

'Well, yes, it's true.'

'She's done it again?' he asked.

I gave no reply.

There he sat for about five minutes, speechless and deep
in thought. Neither Hazay-Hirschfeld nor I spoke a word.
Then Sam spoke to us quietly, almost gaily: 'Will you kindly
wait for me a minute or two?'

'Of course.'

'I'll be back in no time. Only a brief call to Earl F. Millington.'

'What do you want from him?'

'Just to let him know that I'm sailing with him on the
Egalité.'

And he stood up, smiling and looking quite content again,
and walked out to the telephones.

THE LAST SUPPER

I am no mystic. In fact, I am the very opposite of a mystic and talk about premonitions and 'psychic' phenomena either annoys or amuses me. Nor do I claim that I had any premonitions in this particular case, because I just did not. Yet I do not know why I drove down to Southampton to meet the *Egalité*. I have tried to answer this question many times, going over the tiniest and most insignificant details, but I have never been able to find any sort of adequate reason. Sam had not asked me to come; he had thrown out no hint when we were saying goodbye to each other in New York.

Yet, I had no hesitation about going. I watched the huge liner being towed in by tugboats—always a fascinating sight and full of symbolism if you happen to be in the mood for that sort of thing; the giant completely dependent on the skill of dwarfs. The passengers were lining up; there were rows of heads at upper deck portholes. It did not take me long to spot Earl F. Millington who saw me, too, and started waving to me with a broad happy smile.

There was no sign of Sam.

Then I settled down to an endless period of waiting. I knew that passengers had already gone through Immigration—nowadays an immigration officer is always detailed to the onerous duty of crossing the ocean on a luxury liner—but disembarkation and customs, I expected, would take an interminable time. I should have to wait outside that vast, ugly barn of a place until the painstakingly polite yet aloof customs officials had examined countless dirty pants and socks and written out innumerable receipts for the irresistible but utterly useless gadgets people keep bringing home with them from America. I debated with myself whether I should go down to the exit, just in case Sam and Earl F. Millington were among the first to get off, or stay there, on the first floor of the Ocean Terminal for a while, reading the newspaper in a comfortable armchair.

Unexpectedly I heard my name called on the loudspeaker: 'Mr Matyas . . . Will Mr Peter Matyas please report at once at the Inquiry Desk.'

This call filled me with the deepest foreboding. My name is Michael and no one ever called me Peter except, for some unfathomable reason, that one group of American millionaires. Why should they want me on board? And why should Millington summon me instead of Sam?

I hurried to the inquiry desk. A young page boy in his quaint uniform was waiting for me.

'This way, sir,' he said and led me up a small side gangway on to the ship. We made our way through a throng of porters, crew and stewards; not to speak of an endless queue of passengers moving slowly towards the exit. We leapt across barricades of luggage, shipping trunks and sacks of all sizes and colours, we stumbled over overnight air bags, put down carelessly just anywhere. This was essentially an English crowd so there was not much noise, but there was sadness in the air. Journey's end is always a melancholy affair, but the end of an ocean crossing is even worse: you are about to leave a strange and intriguing microcosm where you have been fairly safely isolated from the rest of the world, and to rejoin reality, where you have to tumble over suitcases and kiss relations.

My guide and I left the tumult and proceeded through a deserted corridor. The boy stopped in front of a cabin and knocked.

'*Entrez*,' a voice answered.

We entered the spacious quarters of the First Officer, all heavy furniture, rosewood panelling and about six times as large as one expects a 'cabin' to be. The First Officer was standing behind a massive mahogany table, stiff and unsmiling, with his gold-braided cap on his head. Next to him stood Earl F. Millington.

The First Officer saluted me without uttering a word.

'Oh, Matyas . . .' exclaimed Earl F. Millington. 'How nice to see you, Peter. Boy, am I glad you're here. *Comme ci, comme ça.*'

I stopped and stared at this tableau.

'Gee, am I glad the journey's over.' Then, throwing a quick glance at the officer's marmoreal features, he added quickly: 'Not that this wasn't a pleasant trip. No, sir. It was *very* nice. Really *comme ci, comme ça.* We had a few rough hours but even our Captain could not help that . . .' and he laughed aloud at his wit.

I looked at the First Officer, suspecting that they had other reasons for calling me in than simply to acquaint me with the details of Earl F. Millington's journey, but he went on looking into space with a steely, expressionless gaze. As I was not sure how long Earl F. Millington intended to regale us with his travelogue, I interrupted him rather brusquely: 'Where is Sam?'

He looked at me with surprise: 'In the water.'

'What d'you mean? Having a bath?'

He opened his eyes even more widely, completely taken aback by the fact that I did not already know what he was to tell me.

'Oh, no . . . He's not having a bath. He's buried.'

After a moment's hesitation he added: 'Because he's dead.'

I looked at the officer. He spoke now for the first time—in very correct, very precise English, with just a shade of French accent.

'I'm sorry to have to inform you, that Mr Sam MacKay died on board. At the request of Mr Millington we buried him at sea.'

I was speechless.

I tried to say something but suddenly I felt that uncomfortable lump in my throat of which grown-up men are, as a rule, so much ashamed.

195

The officer spoke again: 'I'll leave you alone, gentlemen. I am sure you wish to hear the details. Please let nothing disturb you. Do you desire a drink?'

'Yes,' I said quickly, 'I do.'

He opened the glass doors of his lavishly equipped cocktail cabinet, made an elegant gesture with his hands, meaning: 'It's all yours,' then went to the door, saluted stiffly and left the room.

I poured a double—perhaps it was a treble—whisky out for myself and gulped it down. I am not much of a drinker but just then I felt I needed it. I pushed the bottle towards Earl F. Millington and he helped himself. Then he said: 'Gee, that man could eat. Myself, I like a good T-bone steak as much as the next guy but gee, I've never seen anything like that fellow Sam.'

He drank a little more whisky.

'If you ask me, Peter, it's kinda unhealthy. It did him no good.'

As the man was lying dead at the bottom of the sea, this sounded a fair assumption.

'Ever heard of a thing called goose-liver? Gee, what he did with that . . . It was real *comme ci, comme ça*.'

I was still stunned by the blow I had just received; thoughts whirled round in my head and I was bursting with impatience to find out what had really happened. Yet—perhaps it was partly the effect of the large dose of whisky—my immediate attention was riveted on Earl F. Millington's curious vocabulary.

'*Comme ci, comme ça*, you said?'

'Sure I did,' he nodded. 'Kinda terrific, if you know what I mean.'

I contemplated him in amazement.

'Well, you can't travel on this blasted boat without picking up a bit of French,' he explained with a modest smile.

'*Comme ci, comme ça*?' I asked, and felt like crying.

'Sure thing,' he agreed.

I heard Earl F. Millington's story; I talked to the First Officer who was not very talkative but who, when he did talk, talked sense; I talked to the Captain, the chef, the ship's doctor, Sam's cabin steward and the night steward. From their accounts a clear picture emerged. It was a story of eating; a story of voracity and mastication. It fell, clearly, into three phases.

At the first two meals on board, Sam had devoured such enormous quantities of food that his fame spread round the ship like wildfire. He wanted to forget his worries, it seemed, he wanted to forget Veronica and his dismissal and was determined to drown his sorrow in grub. Passengers pointed him out to one another and the chef himself sent Sam a message saying that he would be delighted to make his personal acquaintance and so, at Sam's invitation, the chef—a very stout Frenchman, six feet tall, with a round, red, smiling face—came up to the table Sam shared with Earl F. Millington—a rare, if not unprecedented occurrence—and assured Sam that it was an unusual pleasure to meet a real connoisseur on board. He said he would be delighted if Sam would let him know of any special wishes. Sam, who was already half drunk on Poached Turbot followed by Roast Maryland Turkey with Chestnuts, grunted and groaned and said that M. Rotrou, the chef, was very kind indeed. Then he realised that M. Rotrou had no intention of leaving until a 'special wish' was intimated to him.

'We can do everything, M. MacKay,' he said. 'We know all the secrets of Chinese, Russian, Hungarian, Spanish, Persian and Arab cuisine. And needless to say, whatever you can get in France, you can get on the *Egalité*, only much better. What would you like for dinner tonight? What about a *Truite de Rivière Grillée Normande*? Or just an Omelette Jessica? You must try our Omelette Jessica, Monsieur.'

And M. Rotrou gave a loud, smacking kiss to the tips of his three fingers.

'Or why don't you try our Prague Ham? I mean, of course, Prague Ham *en Saulpiquet Montbardois*. . . .'

Sam was unmoved.

'Got any goose-liver?' he asked.

'Pâté?'

'No. Simple goose-liver.'

M. Rotrou was deeply disappointed. They had the best Strasbourg goose-liver, needless to say, but he wanted to cook, to prepare something. 'Goose-liver,' he nodded grimly and left.

That evening an artistic masterpiece was delivered at their table on a large, gleaming trolley; a superb swan-like goose made of ice, swimming on a salver which looked like a silver lake. Colourful silk ribbons were used as decoration and the goose had two green eyes made of what Sam and Earl F. Millington took to be real emeralds. In the goose's back was a cavity in which were nicely placed three exquisitely thin slices of goose-liver, obviously cut with a razor blade. Sam glared at this apparition for a long time with mounting anger. He beckoned to the steward: 'Send Michael Angelo in!'

'Michael Angelo, Monsieur?'

'Yes. M. Rotrou, the chef.'

It was a most unusual request. M. Rotrou was a V.I.P. whom even the Captain treated with the utmost respect and who could not be just sent for. But M. Rotrou thought Sam wanted to express gratitude coupled with delighted adulation, so he came.

'I said goose-liver, M. Rotrou,' Sam bawled at him. 'Goose-liver. If I want a statue, I go to St Peter's in Rome. I go to Florence. I go to the Musée Rodin. Cut out the fine art, Rotrou. Leave that to Sir Henry Moore. Or Sir Michael Angelo. All I want from you is goose-liver. Lots of it, without statues, pictures, symphonies or sonatas.'

M. Rotrou, flaming red in the face, bowed and moved away with as much dignity as he could muster. A few minutes later a whole, huge goose-liver was served to Sam on a thick dinner plate, covered with a checked red-and-white napkin. This was

M. Rotrou's subtle retort expressive of his contempt for a man who preferred vulgar belly-fodder to the fine arts. The subtle nature of the retort was completely lost on Sam, who devoured the goose-liver at breathtaking speed—minus one single slice which he offered to Earl F. Millington.

'Anything to drink, Monsieur?' asked the wine steward, when Sam was nearly through his liver.

'Just a little Saint Nectaire,' he replied.

The wine steward was taken aback.

'Saint Nectaire, Monsieur?'

'Yes.'

'But Saint Nectaire is a cheese, Monsieur.'

'I know,' nodded Sam thoughtfully. 'I am not very keen on alcohol, you see. After a goose-liver I always drink a bit of cheese.'

This painful scene with M. Rotrou inaugurated the second phase of Sam's eating orgy. Next morning he sent a message to Rotrou, saying that he wished to apologise for his rudeness and would be greatly honoured if the chef would come up to the bar to have an apéritif with him. A sullen, sulking, red-faced Rotrou appeared to tell Sam that he could have no drinks at the bar, but Sam flattered him with great charm, all was forgiven in no time and, whatever the regulations might say, drinks were ordered.

'You said you knew the cuisine of all nations, M. Rotrou, didn't you?'

'That's my speciality, Monsieur,' replied Rotrou proudly. 'Whatever you can think of. Vietnamese, then what people call Chinese and you and I know is really Cantonese; Andalusian. Moroccan, Texan. If you like Argentine baby-beef, Monsieur . . .'

'I think you also mentioned Hungarian food?'

'But of course. Do you like paprika chicken? Or stuffed pepper? Or if you prefer that great delicacy, the fish called *fogas* of Lake Balaton—well, you can have it with béchamel sauce.'

'Have you ever heard of plum-dumplings, M. Rotrou?'

The chef's face fell.

'Plum-dumplings?'

'Yes. Plum-dumplings.'

'I can't say I have heard of them. I can look it up though. We can make everything, M. MacKay. Everything.'

'Good. That's what I'd like for dinner tonight.'

'And what else? This is a sweet if I'm not mistaken.'

'Your knowledge is most impressive, M. Rotrou and, of course, you are not mistaken. But I'll have nothing else. I want fifty-one plum-dumplings, that's all.'

'Fifty-one?' asked M. Rotrou with growing agitation.

'Fifty-one, M. Rotrou.'

'Not fifty? Or fifty-two? Just fifty-one?'

'If you give me fifty-two, I'll leave one. If you give me fifty, I'll leave the table hungry.'

Sam had his fifty-one plum-dumplings for dinner. He managed to eat them all. 'At least I have achieved *something* in life,' he commented to Earl F. Millington. He felt so ill that night that his groans alerted the night steward, who called the doctor.

'Have you ever had any trouble with your heart?' asked the doctor.

'Never.'

'Not even slight discomfort?'

'Not the slightest.'

'You may call yourself lucky. Take one of these now,' and he fished some medicine out of his bag, 'and two more after breakfast. You must take it very easy tomorrow. A cup of tea for breakfast and nothing else; a cup of tea with a piece of toast— but no butter remember—for lunch and another cup of tea and dry toast for dinner.'

'Yes,' nodded Sam. 'Tea and dry toast, I understand.'

'You must follow my instructions. It might prove dangerous if you don't.'

Next day Sam ate two roast chickens for lunch and, as he had asked M. Rotrou the previous day to prepare some *sholet* for him, he felt that he could not let the chef down. So he ate such an amount of *sholet* that the mere sight of it made Earl F. Millington violently sick. He was up all night. Sam, however, slept like a baby.

The next day saw the third and, as it turned out, the last phase of Sam's orgy. At lunch time he disciplined himself to some extent, ate very little and—for the first and last time during the voyage—had half a bottle of wine, some Puilly-Fuissé with his modest meal. But at dinner time he went berserk and started devouring food in a manner in which he had never eaten before in his life. He ordered one dish after another; soup after hors d'oeuvre, fish after eggs, meat after a grill; touched everything, tasted everything, then left it to turn his greedy, avid attention to the next plate. Was it thus that Veronica had tasted all men, once upon a time? Or did he feel that he must enjoy all the food there was on this ship—and all the food (and food, perhaps, means love) there was in the world—because he would never have another chance of doing so? He had some green olives with celery first, then caviar, then a mixed hors d'oeuvre, then turtle soup with Swiss cheese and then a few Canapés Beauharnais . . . He left more than half of everything but as he went on, his appetite seemed to increase and so did his excitement. He had *Oeufs Cocotte Périgueux*—he asked for three eggs, specifically, but hardly ate more than half an egg—and then he ordered cold Scotch salmon, roast saddle of lamb *Jardin d'Egalité* and broiled New Jersey chicken with bacon. . . . Then he asked for a baked apple in jelly, but by the time it arrived he was leaning across the table, gasping for air and moaning with pain.

'Are you all right, Sam?' asked Earl F. Millington.

Sam gave no reply.

'You sure have a hearty appetite,' remarked Earl F.

Sam fell forward and started to breathe stertorously.

'I'll call the doctor,' said Millington.

Sam raised his head.

'What?' he asked in a drunken stupor.

'I'll call the doctor.'

Sam gave him a vacant look.

'The doctor,' Earl F. Millington repeated.

At the back of his mind Sam was vaguely aware that he was supposed to be dining on tea and toast—without butter.

'No,' he said quietly and quite soberly. 'Not the doctor. I'm all right. Really, I am.'

He stood up but lost his balance and fell down, all his length, and lay there, between the tables. A few stewards and passengers jumped to help him. There was some commotion but Sam was up on his feet again, thanked everyone, and assured them he was quite all right. In fact, he looked all right.

'Give me a hand to my cabin, Earl. I'll be perfectly all right tomorrow morning.'

He leaned a little on Millington but walked mainly by his own efforts. When he reached his cabin—or 'stateroom' as it is called under strong American influence—he reassured Millington that he needed no help and he would get to bed on his own.

He did.

He left his door unlocked.

Next morning, the steward found him dead. He was lying in bed, wearing his pyjamas and a happy smile played round his lips. He must have dreamt of plum-dumplings; his face looked like one.

He had died in his sleep.

3

'He asked me in New York before he embarked, when he was filling up some papers,' Earl F. Millington told me, 'if I minded if he gave my name as his next-of-kin. You've got to put someone on those papers, as you know. "I can't name Mariska as I left her; and I can't name Veronica who is enjoying herself in

Barbados with Sir Henry Salami. I want you, Earl"—that's what he said. I told him: "Sure, it's O.K., Sammy, go ahead." I never gave the matter another thought until he was found dead and these guys came to me and asked what I wanted to do with Sam's body. Well, I told them I didn't want to do anything with it. Nothing at all. I liked Sammy, sure I did, but what could I do with his dead body?

'They told me it could be embalmed—they have a first-class embalmer on board. Imagine, they carry an embalmer who does as good a job as anyone in New York. Other times he works in the butcher-shop, in the store-room—there are not enough passengers to be embalmed to give him a full time job—but he's a top guy, they assured me. Yessir, he is. They said they would land the body at Southampton, or Cherbourg, if I preferred, but we decided to bury him at sea.

'There was a post-mortem and the doctor who signed the death certificate said he had died in his sleep of heart failure probably caused by overeating. Well, we suspected as much as that. The Captain gave permission for the burial.

'Well, about the funeral: there were a number of priests on board—there were all sorts of services every day, occupying the main library and interfering with bingo—and all these priest guys starting quarrelling because all of them wanted to bury Sam. But no one was quite certain what his religion was. It seems he'd met a man on the first day and they had a chat on religion on the Promenade Deck and Sam informed him he was a Seventh Day Adventist. But he told someone else that he was a Jehovah's Witness. He told the Roman Catholic priest that he was a Shintoist, but I know that he was pulling everybody's leg because he was a Buddhist.'

'A Buddhist?' I asked. Earl F. Millington never lost his power of surprising me.

'Sure thing,' he nodded knowledgeably. 'He told me himself, confidentially. I told him I never knew Hungarians were Buddhists, and he explained that as a rule they were not, but he had come from a Buddhist district in North Hungary—or maybe he said South Hungary. Well, Shintoist or Buddhist, I said, a non-denominational Christian burial would cover both.

'So he was buried by the Captain himself. These sailor guys don't like people dying on board, it's bad for business, so they arranged the funeral for four o'clock in the morning. I ask you... First I flatly refused to attend at that ungodly hour, at the crack of dawn, but they said I was next-of-kin, the most important person, so I thought to hell with it. Four in the morning, if you please. There were only a few members of the crew present and about half a dozen passengers, it's amazing at what time some people will get up for a little fun. The Captain said the prayers very nicely, all in French, it was very *comme ci, comme ça*, except that he must have had a few quick ones and he was quite drunk if you ask me. His speech was a bit slurred and he hiccupped three times while saying the Lord's Prayer, but it was a really moving ceremony, kinda dignified, if you know what I mean. .... Then the Captain pushed a button and one end of the coffin rose and it started sliding down on some rails on a kind of chute. Well, sir, they think of everything on these modern liners. The equipment they carry! That's what I call modern comfort. This was on the Boat Deck, you see, one of the lower decks, very near the water. The coffin moved slowly at first, but then faster and faster. They'd removed a section of the rails. There was a big splash and the coffin floated for a moment on the surface and then disappeared and that was the end of Sam and we all went in to have a drink and we needed it too. Yessir, I can tell you that. ....

'This morning they presented me with the bill for the whole show. It's not cheap at all—but far the cheapest. Embalming would have cost a great deal more. I paid the bill all right, but I'll get the money back from T.C.C. It was legitimate business expense, after all, don't you agree?'

'You don't think he committed suicide?' I asked him.

'What?'

'Suicide.'

'Good God, no! He died a natural death. I've told you.

Perhaps you did not notice what I said. He died of heart failure in his sleep. He was full of beans right to the last minute. Full of *joie de vivre*, if you know this expression. Enjoyed his food. Every bit of it. Gee, that guy could eat.'

'He could, no doubt. . . . He never told you that he was fed up with life or anything like that?'

'Oh, no. On the contrary. He kept joking all the time—you knew him. He said that the art of dying was much finer and more important than the art of living. He also said once that he did not mind if his standard of living had occasionally been very low as long as his standard of dying remained high.'

'He said that?'

'Yes. But apart from silly jokes like that he said nothing. Nothing at all. He could not mean much by these, because he was happy and contented all the time. Real *comme ci, comme ça.*'

'You know, it was just after he had some terrible news that he changed his air ticket for this boat?'

'I surely don't know about that. If you mean his job and his wife—well, he kept joking about them, too, and didn't take them seriously at all. He came by boat, he told me, because he wanted to enjoy my company. I flatter myself by believing him.'

'And you know, Earl, that he had had a severe heart attack and that he knew perfectly well that excessive eating . . . Well, it doesn't really matter. Let's forget about it. There is only one more thing I want to ask you.'

'Go ahead. Shoot.'

'Why did you have him buried at sea?'

'Why? Now, you caught me. You ask me why I wanted to have him buried at sea?'

'Yes. Why?'

'It was on my advice, Monsieur,' the First Officer butted in seriously.

I had quite forgotten that he had returned to his róom, where we were now talking.

'Yours?'

'Mine. It was because of something Mr MacKay said to Mr Millington.'

'Sure it was,' said Earl F. Millington, embarrassed. 'That last night, when I helped him to his cabin, he made a most peculiar remark.'

I waited in silence.

Earl F. Millington continued reluctantly: 'He made one of his little jokes. I shouldn't have taken any notice of it.'

'What did he say?' I asked impatiently.

'He said: "I've loved a good meal all my life; I want to end up as a good meal." When I asked him what the devil he meant, he smiled and replied: "I've loved fish all my life; I'm sure the fish will love me." '

'He said that?' I asked, horrified.

'Yes. . . . And the First Officer, when I told him . . . he thought . . . he suggested . . .'

'I regarded this as a personal wish expressed by the deceased,' said the First Officer.

But Earl F. Millington was still unconvinced.

'I'm not sure I did the right thing.'

'Yes, you did the right thing,' said I.

4

Mariska returned to Miss Markos and her mother. They'd kept her place for her, partly for old times' sake, and partly because any other maid would have cost six times as much.

Veronica, on learning the tragic news, immediately broke with Sir Henry Salami and spent years in deep mourning. She does not look at any man—even today—five years after Sam's death. She can be faithful to a shadow and to a memory if, alas, to no flesh-and-blood male.

The Trust for Christian Civilisation carries on its beneficial activities on a vastly increased scale. They have turned completely Afro-Asian. They have just had the complete works of

Ben Jonson, Jane Austen and James Mitchener translated into Ibibio and 200,000 copies of them have been distributed in Zanzibar, where no one speaks Ibibio. Now—under the imprint of the Wyoming University Press—they are preparing an anthology of Katangese poetry, selected and translated into English by Bubuye Liyinkambo. Professor Hazay-Hirschfeld and Crispian Ransome-Hall have already declared that, under certain conditions, they might be prepared to take over 20,000 copies of this anthology for Szeged University, free of charge. In T.C.C. circles, this is regarded as a roaring success and there is much mutual congratulation.

In short, they are all frantically busy and have long ago forgotten their founder, Sam MacKay.